MY ONLY SIN IS MY CASTE

VIKAS RAY

Invincible Publishers

First published in India in 2019

ISBN : 978-93-88333-81-8

Invincible Publishers

Registered Address: 201A, SAS Tower, Sector 38,
Gurgaon-122003

Printed at Thomson Press (India) LTD

Dedicated To The Brahmin Girl, Whom I Love

- A Yadav Boy

Table of Contents

Part I

September, 2016

"This is my last warning to you, Vihaan," the stern bespectacled landlord said. "You can't do your singing practice after eight every night. My daughter's studies are getting affected. I had warned you when letting you the apartment that you are not allowed to do anything that disturbs us."

Vihaan's hands balled into a fist in a barely suppressed rage. He had had enough of this; getting bullied for no reason by this burly landlord. Before he could think better, he blurted, "Fine, I'm vacating the house then. No matter what I do, I end up disturbing your family. I'd rather stay on the footpath than be the cause of your headache." Vihaan's thin, boyish face had turned red in anger.

The landlord's temper seeped out in a second. "No! No! I didn't mean that."

Vihaan smiled sarcastically. "Don't worry, uncle. I know the rent you get from me helps you run the household. But since I'm disturbing you so much, I'd rather leave. I shouldn't bother anyone unnecessarily."

"Vihaan...I..." the landlord spluttered.

"You won't be bothered by me from tomorrow." With that Vihaan picked up his laptop bag from the study table and strode out of the apartment triumphantly, reveling in the deathly blow he had landed on his troublesome, meddling landlord.

It was only when he was on the bus, getting crushed between two sweaty and beefy men, did the repercussions of his hasty words dawned on him. He would be homeless if he left the apartment in Mulund. It was almost after a year of staying in various hostels and PG that he had got this one BHK apartment for himself within his budget where he could live on his own, and host his family and friends when they came to visit. That was one of the reasons why he loved having a house of his own. He loved to play host. He had spent his whole life in small, rented houses where six members of his family had to be squeezed in. Now that he was being able to give some semblance of comfort to his family when they came to him, he enjoyed a feeling of achievement.

But Vihaan was a man of his words. True, he didn't think through before saying that he would move out. But now that the words were out, he couldn't see how he could back out without losing his self-respect. This was his problem—his short-temper. From his school to his college, to his university, and now at work—he was infamous for his short-temper. He had always been a very cute-looking boy. Girls always got attracted to him at the very first sight. But then after a few dates, they would start to face his anger issues, and they would run; in the opposite direction. After every bad experience, he promised to himself that he would learn to control himself, but he slipped up every time. But this time he realized he had bitten off more than he could chew.

He was extremely edgy by the time he reached his office at Airoli, Navi Mumbai. When he received a memo to attend a team meeting in the afternoon, his mind was hardly into it. Instead, he went out to the corridor to call his broker who informed him without any pretense that he couldn't arrange a house for him in one day. Vihaan was not a smoker by habit. But he did like a few drags now and then to calm his nerves whenever he got into difficult situations. Thus, craving for a smoke, he went out to buy cigarettes from the paan shop across from his office building.

Instead of buying just one or two cigarettes, Vihaan bought an entire packet. He walked to a cluster of trees that were used as a shade and stood there smoking. Now that his broker had given up, he had to search elsewhere. He went online on his mobile and started checking the available properties for rent. But nothing seemed to fit the bill.

He was thinking about discussing the matter with some of his colleagues. Maybe they knew of some place where he could move in at such short notice. He was trying to make a mental list of all the people who he could probably approach for help, and it wasn't long before Abhishek arrived there and his eyes fell on Vihaan. Abhishek got some sandwiches from a food stall and came to stand with Vihaan.

"Hey, man, what's up with you? The finance support team is having a tough time finishing all the mini-projects within the deadline. And, here you are, the rising star of the team, hiding here and smoking." Abhishek held out a sandwich to Vihaan. "Girlfriend ditched?"

"No, dude! I don't have a girlfriend." Vihaan refused the sandwich that Abhishek was offering with the gesture of his hand, "Not hungry."

Abhishek guffawed but checked himself quickly. "Sorry, about that." He took a bite of the sandwich. "But seriously, how come you don't have a girlfriend? How do you live like that? I mean...you know...the cravings?"

Vihaan shot Abhishek a disgusted look. "I need to think about the roof over my head right now."

"Why? The landlord threw you out?" Abhishek continued chewing his sandwich nonchalantly.

"No. I ditched my landlord."

That got Abhishek's attention and he fixed Vihaan with an overtly curious gaze. "How come?"

"His family doesn't approve of my singing practise."

Abhishek goggled at Vihaan, momentarily at a loss for words. "Uh! Singing practise! Who are you? Sonu Nigam? You do resemble him any bit? But seriously. This is funny!"

"Yeah, funny!" Vihaan snapped. "I can't stop laughing, dude." Vihaan strode away, leaving Abhishek gobsmacked.

Everyone was like Abhishek, Vihaan thought bitterly as he took the lift to the eighth floor. Nobody understood or supported his passion for music. And he didn't want to sit and explain himself to anybody.

An hour later, Vihaan was in the conference room with the members of two different teams–sales and finance. The two team leads were also present along with their associate manager. Vihaan could hardly focus on anything that was being said at the beginning of the meeting. Excelor had obtained a new project for which they would be coordinating with their foreign offices. The associate manager was briefing about the project. Vihaan knew they would have an in-depth presentation later so he let his mind wander back to his immediate worries.

After about an hour of droning on, the associate manager stopped briefly to drink some water, and Vihaan's eyes went around the room, taking in the less-than-enthusiastic expressions on his colleague's faces. It seemed no one else was much interested in the briefing either. It was then that his eyes fell on Tisha who was sitting opposite him, towards the end of the long conference table. Her eyes were red and her lips were trembling. Vihaan couldn't look away.

Tisha Shukla was a level above Vihaan in the designation. Tisha was the Application Development Senior Analyst in the sales support team, while Vihaan was the Application Development Analyst in finance support. She had been working at Excelor for four years, while Vihaan had been there for three. They never had much chance of becoming friends, though Vihaan found Tisha very pretty. Tisha sat across from him in the aisle beside his, and the only contact they have had in the last three years was during the Fun Fridays and in the Townhall.

The most they had talked was if they had bumped into each other on their way;that too formal greetings, never anything personal. But the whole office, including Vihaan, knew that Tisha was in a relationship with Rehan Verma, another guy from the sales support team.

Tisha was glancing every now and then at Rehan who was sitting at the head of the table, right beside the associate manager. Vihaan could easily guess the source of her trouble. She must have been having a tiff with Rehan.

Before Vihaan could think too much about Tisha's issues, the associate manager gathered himself and announced with the air of Father Christmas pulling out a toy from his sack, "You would be thrilled to know that three people would be sent to our client site located in London at the end of this year, and they would work from there till the completion of their assigned duties on this project." He cleared his throat, dragging the moment of suspense, for every person in the room was now alert and gave him their undivided attention. "After the review of past performances, the management has chosen the most eligible candidates for the client site stint; Mr. Maroof Sheikh from sales support!"

The room bursted into a polite applause for Maroof who beamed around at everyone.

"Ms. Tisha Shukla, also from sales support."

Tisha was more shocked than pleased. Her eyes darted towards Rehan at the very mention of her name, and she gave him a tremulous smile. Rehan nodded at her slightly without showing much enthusiasm. More applause followed for Tisha. She was even thumped on the back by her team members. She was clearly popular among her team.

"The last member..." the associate manager continued, drawing everyone's eyes towards him again, "...is Mr. Vihaan Kumar."

Vihaan ogled at the associate manager, sure that his ears were malfunctioning. He had never even gone on holidays to faraway places, and now he going was to London for a year. Vihaan was hardly able to react with proper enthusiasm as his teammates congratulated him happily. As everyone shook his hand, Vihaan's eyes fell on Tisha who was staring at him with her big, pointed eyes. His heart fluttered for a moment as their eyes met. Tisha smiled at him, and he smiled back quite involuntarily, his victory sicking in finally.

The rest of the day passed in a frenzy of work and celebration. It was nearing the month end, and Vihaan was on a tight budget, but he still gave a nice treat to his teammates at the fourth-floor cafeteria when they converged on him, demanding a celebration. In all the hullabaloo, Vihaan didn't get a chance to discuss his accommodation issue with anyone. With the excitement around him and inside him, he could hardly focus on his problem the entire day. He just couldn't wait to go back home and get his whole family on the conference call and share the news with them.

It was late in the evening when Vihaan was in the cafeteria again, listening to Maroon 5 songs on his Ipad. By then he had accepted defeat. He was quite prepared to lose face in front of his landlord. He noticed Tisha come and sit at the table beside him. They exchanged a small smile, the usual gesture between them for the last three years.

Vihaan kept glancing at Tisha out of the corner of his eyes. He saw her order spaghetti pasta with cold coffee. She kept calling someone from her mobile, but soon she grew frustrated and kept her mobile back into her bag. Vihaan sat nibbling on his friend Maggi, trying not to look at Tisha. She was petite atfive feet two inches, and very cute. She got dimples when she smiled, he had noticed that earlier in the day. His mind went back to wondering about Tisha's relationship with Rehan. They were the perfect couple. If he ever had a relationship, he wanted it to be like that of Tisha and Rehan.

All of a sudden, he heard Tisha's muffled voice, as if she was talking to him. "Mr. Kumar, are you showing off?"

Vihaan looked around at her, taken aback. Tisha was staring right at him. Vihaan took off the earphones. "Did you say something?" he asked.

"Are you showing off?" Tisha repeated herself. "Who listens to English songs? We are Indians. What's better than Bollywood for us, huh?"

Vihaan was momentarily lost at words. "It's nothing like that."

But then Tisha cracked a cheeky smile on seeing his dumbfounded expression. "Relax, I'm kidding. I also like Maroon 5. Anyway, congratulations. We'll be going to London together later this year."

This thought had been going on in Vihaan's mind all day, and he automatically smiled at Tisha, "Yes. Congratulations to you, too." He extended his hand towards Tisha. Tisha shook hands with him. Her hand was soft, and Vihaan felt something deep stir in the pit of his stomach at her touch. They held each other's eyes for a moment, and then quickly let go of each other. Tisha smiled at him again and got up with her empty plate. Vihaan sat there for the next ten minutes, smiling to himself like an idiot. He had no idea why he was getting happy about going to London with someone else's girlfriend.

It was quite late at night when Vihaan was waiting at the auto stand. The queue for the auto was very long, and Vihaan was getting irritated. The autos were arriving at the stand almost at ten to fifteen minutes' intervals. At this rate, Vihaan was sure it would be past ten before he could reach home.

Suddenly, Tisha stopped her scooty in front of Vihaan, "Hey, Mr. Kumar, waiting for an auto?"

"Yeah, but it doesn't seem like I'll be getting one soon tonight."

"Where do you live?" Tisha asked.

"Mulund West."

"Oh! Hey, I live in Bhandup. It's like a fifteen-minute distance. Wow! We live so close and we never knew of that."

Vihaan became unusuallyaware of everyone in the queue staring at them. But Tisha seemed oblivious to all the staring. "You must be getting late? Do you want a lift?"

Vihaan nodded like a punch drunk, still unable to process what was happening.

"Hop on then," Tisha said invitingly.

Vihaan climbed behind Tisha. He hesitated about placing his hand on Tisha while Tisha asked, "Are you ready? Should we go?" Vihaan stammered incoherently, "Yeah..." and before he could steady himself Tisha was off. Startled, Vihaan was jerked into Tisha and as their bodies collided Vihaan felt his breath catch in his chest. But again, Tisha was oblivious to everything. In fact, she was enjoying the ride.

"Hold on, Mr. Kumar. I like to ride fast," Tisha said over the sound of the rushing wind. She was going so fast that Vihaan felt his heart drum inside his heart.

"Have you got a death wish?" Vihaan almost screamed into her ear.

Tisha laughed. "I don't believe in dying. We are born to live and that's what I'm doing right now."

It was an intense twenty-minute ride during which Vihaan didn't dare to say another word to Tisha, scared of diverting her attention and getting into an accident. By the time Tisha was dropping him in front of his apartment, Vihaan was quite sure that the Tisha in office and the Tisha on the roads were two strangers. The girl he had known for three years was soft and demure. And, the one he was with tonight was daring and carefree.

"Did you enjoy that?" Tisha asked with an excited smile.

"I'm a very boring guy, Tisha. I like to move at more humanly speeds."

Tisha pouted like a petulant child. "So, this is the thank you I'm going to get?"

Vihaan felt a tug in his heart on seeing the mock anger on Tisha's beautiful face. "Thank you, Tisha. It was really kind of you to help me out tonight."

"I want a treat tomorrow," Tisha demanded suddenly.

Vihaan was more than willing to oblige the pretty girl who had just helped him out, "Sure."

Tisha smiled. "You are sweet."

They both heard the sound of someone clearing his throat from behind. They both looked around. The landlord was standing at the main gate and looking daggers at them. He came towards Vihaan as Vihaan's insides sank in trepidation.

"So, young man, are you staying or leaving?" the landlord demanded to know without beating about the bush.

Vihaan wished Tisha wasn't there to witness his humiliation. However, he gritted his teeth before answering. "I'll move out as soon as I get another place."

The landlord gave him a dirty smile triumphantly. "Getting a place to stay isn't so easy, is it? Shouldn't you respect those who trust you with their property?" He turned towards Tisha and gave her an ingratiating smile. "What do you think?"

Tisha fixed the landlord with a beady look, assessing him for a moment.

Vihaan addressed Tisha, realizing that Tisha needed to leave before things got ugly. "You should leave. I'll catch up with you tomorrow."

Tisha didn't' seem to hear him. "Do you need someplace to move into?"

"No, he doesn't," the landlord answered out of turn.

"Vihaan?" Tisha disregarded the landlord like he was a stretch of wall.

Vihaan wasn't sure why Tisha was asking him that question so confidently, so he answered in an off-handed way, "Yes. But I think you should leave now."

"I have an idea," Tisha said. "I have an ex-colleague from Excelor. I'm not sure if you know him. Siddharth?"

Vihaan nodded, remembering a friendly guy he had met in the first six months of his tenure at Excelor. "Yeah. What about him?"

"He stays nearby. His wife has gone out for a few days. I'm sure he won't mind letting you crash at his place for two or three days. You can make other arrangements in the meantime."

Vihaan looked awestruck at Tisha. It seemed to him like he had never really noticed her properly before. She seemed to have a twinkle in her eyes; something he had never noticed before in anyone else. For a moment he was lost in her eyes.

"Vihaan?" Tisha had to bring him back to planet Earth.

"Yeah, that would be great if he agrees," Vihaan said enthusiastically. He looked at the crestfallen landlord.

Tisha took out her mobile from her laptop bag and rang Siddharth. A smile unfurled on her lips as she talked to him for a few minutes and explained the whole situation. Rather than focussing on what she was saying on the phone, his concentration was on her lips. The more he looked at her lips, the more he wanted to kiss her.

"It's settled," Tisha announced happily after disconnecting the call. "Go and get your things. I'll drop you to Siddharth's place."

Vihaan turned to the devastated landlord. "Wait for a bit, uncle," Vihaan said with relish. "I'll get the money from the ATM and clear the rent for this month."

The landlord could only shoot both of them a nasty glare as Vihaan climbed behind Tisha on her scooty again. "Can you take me to the ATM first?"

"Yup. Hold on tight." And, they were off, Vihaan truly enjoying the mad ride this time around.

Within the next two hours, Vihaan was settled at Siddharth's place, and Siddharth was insisting Tisha to stay back for dinner. Initially, Tisha was reluctant, but when Vihaan also started insisting her to stay, she finally relented. Siddharth ordered some Chinese online and they sat talking into the night over dinner. The focus of the dinner-time discussion was of course on Vihaan.

"You said you'd move out just because he was complaining about your singing lessons. Really?" Tisha asked, surprised. "You love singing that much?"

Vihaan got defensive immediately. "Yes, I do."

Tisha didn't laugh. Instead, she looked impressed. "You know what I did in school? I wanted to go to a dance competition. But there was a class test that day in school. So mom wouldn't allow me to go for it and dropped me to school herself. I went inside with everybody else, and then jumped out of the window of the girl's toilet, and ran out of the school from the back gate."

Tisha grinned at Vihaan and extended her raised hand towards him for a high-five. "For crazy passion!" Vihaan smiled happily and slapped her hand in celebration. They had found a friend in each other.

By the time Tisha went back to her place and Vihaan was exhausted by the day's events and crashed on the couch in the drawing room of Siddharth's apartment. Vihaan wished Rehan was not there in the picture. But then he remembered how Tisha had smiled happily at Rehan the moment she had heard of her success, and all hope drained out of his heart. But at least, he had found a kindred spirit in her. He let that thought lull him into sleep.

Part II

Vihaan reached office early, buoyed up by his broker's promise that he would get him a new place within a week at most. Hardly anyone had come into the office by then, and the few people who had arrived were milling around, drinking coffee or chatting on their phones. Vihaan's eyes were drawn towards Tisha's empty seat every now and then. He couldn't wait to see her and thank her again. His teammates started arriving one by one and they greeted each other warmly. These people, Aanchal, Mohit, Abhishek, and Sourav, had become something like his family. All of them were living alone in Mumbai for their jobs, and they all had come to depend on each other.

Once Vihaan and his teammates were done discussing their jobs for the day, the conversation smoothly transitioned into a personal space. Vihaan narrated the thrilling adventure he had last night. They all knew how much Vihaan hated his landlord and they were happy for him. They also promised to help him look for a new place. But what interested Vihaan's teammates the most was Tisha's involvement in the whole thing.

Aanchal seemed to be most intrigued by Tisha, "She is a nice girl. She talks to everyone politely. But I never imagined she could be so bold and, you know, helpful, I guess you can call it that."

Sourav scoffed, "Big deal! When has one girl seen anything good in another girl?"

Aanchal swelled with indignation. "What does that mean? You think I'm being jealous?"

Vihaan quickly intervened before things could get heated up. "Hey! hey guys! come on! Don't behave like kids now."

Aanchal and Sourav gave each other the evil eye and went back to their work stations. Vihaan shot one last look at Tisha's empty seat before starting with his work. Tisha had asked for a treat, and he wondered what he could do for her that would please her. But as he sat making plans inside his head, the pleasantness of his thoughts was stopped short by the ugly realization that he could not get too close with Tisha, otherwise, Rehan could get offended. Right as he realized did his heart sink at the thought and he saw Tisha arrive. She settled down and gave a small wave at Vihaan, but Vihaan returned her cheerful smile only half-heartedly. Tisha's smile faltered at his lukewarm greeting. Vihaan noticed that and hastily turned to his computer monitor.

He spent the rest of the day trying not to pay any attention to Tisha. He had had enough heartbreaks; he didn't want any drama at the office. But for some reason, he couldn't help his eyes move towards Tisha's desk every so often. Sometimes, Tisha would be biting a pencil while focusing on her monitor, sometimes she would be on her phone, sometimes she would be chatting with her teammates. Vihaan couldn't help noticing how beautiful she looked. She was dressed simply in a salwar-kameez and had dainty earrings on. The whole effect was mesmerizing. Tisha's sight interested Vihaan more than his work that day, and he kept feeling guilty for not responding to her properly in the morning.

Vihaan was in the cafeteria, eating his lunch in the afternoon. He had seen while leaving for lunch that Tisha was still at her desk, working away furiously on her computer. He wondered if she would get free anytime soon. Just when he was about to go up after getting an urgent call from his manager, he saw Tisha arrive with her teammate, Prerna. She didn't notice him as she and Prerna took a seat. He had a sudden idea. He went up to the man at the food counter and pointed out Tisha to him. "Please give her a Dairy Milk Silk." He paid for the chocolate and walked away.

Five minutes later Vihaan went back to his desk and logged into his account again. It was while shifting his keyboard around that a small piece of paper fell from under the keyboard. He picked it up and saw a small handwritten note on it:

'Y so grumpy, Mr. Singer? I wanna hear wat happnd. Call me when u hv tym. 9167535151'

A wide smile spread on Vihaan's face as he stared at the note for a while. He was sure it was from Tisha. He quickly saved her number on his mobile and texted her:

Njy ur lunch...ttyl. Hv to run for a meeting.

The reply came within a minute.

It would have been nice if u had stayed and given me d treat in person. Anyway, thnx. Have a gud day.

Vihaan's smile only widened.

Nxt tym. U hv a gud day too.

Vihaan was happy to know that Tisha appreciated his gesture. But then he wondered if Tisha had told Rehan anything about last night. He looked around the office and found Rehan working busily at his desk. A strange ominous feeling came over him. He did not want to be the source of any trouble in Tisha's life, and so he resolved not to ping Tisha of his own volition. After that decision, he almost forced Tisha out of his mind.

It was around eleven at night. Siddharth had gone to bed. Vihaan had just finished talking to his family members. He had finally told them about his client site posting. So, after a long gap, he went on his blog and tried to write a poem. Writing poems whenever the mood struck was another one of his hobbies, just like music. He wanted to write something happy, something about the brightness of life. But his thoughts kept going back to Tisha. And, words flowed into his mind. His hands started moving across the keypad as Tisha's face swam in front of his eyes.

As if by some telepathic means, the moment Vihaan published the new poem on his blog, Tisha's call came through. Vihaan's heart thudded excitedly as he saw her name flashing on his mobile screen. He had resolved not to make the first move, but that didn't mean he had to avoid Tisha when she was eager to come towards him. With slight trepidation, he received the call.

"Hi, Vihaan. Am I disturbing you?" Tisha chirped over the phone.

"Nope. In fact, you called at a very good time."

"Really? What happened?"

"I just wrote a new poem for my blog. Would you like to check it out?"

"You write also?" Tisha's voice held awe.

Vihaan said a little smugly, "A little bit."

"Can I see what your 'little bit' is like?"

"Sure." Vihaan was suddenly nervous. He was going to show Tisha the poem that he had written for her. He wondered if she would guess that she was his muse. "But I don't think this one has turned out all that well," Vihaan said in a half-hearted attempt to dissuade her.

"Let me decide that," Tisha said adamantly. "What's your blog called?"

"Zindagi."

"Fine then. I'll check it out and call you back in five minutes. Send me the link." She disconnected the call.

Vihaan sent her the link feeling extremely nervous. Then he waited anxiously for Tisha to call back. Unable to keep still, he got up from the couch and went to stand by the window. In less than three minutes Tisha rang again. “Hey, we have an in-house poet, and none of us knew that. That’s a shame! So, who’s the girl?”

“Girl? What girl?” Vihaan floundered nervously.

“The girl you wrote about. Who’s she?”

Vihaan was afraid of this very question. “Priyanka Chopra,” he blurted out.

Tisha guffawed. “Really? What are you? A school kid?”

“Yeah, so I fantasize about the hottest girl in the country. Big deal!” Vihaan pretended to be indignant, knowing completely well how silly he was sounding.

“Oops! You are getting angry. Okay, okay, let’s get serious,” Tisha hastily backtracked. “Is everything all right for you at work? You looked disturbed.”

Vihaan’s heart melted instantly on hearing the concern in her voice. “No no, it’s fine. Just a little hectic at the moment.”

“That’s good. We are also struggling with so much overload. I think our team has to work overtime this weekend. I hate working on weekends.”

“I see.”

“Yeah, and how are you doing in Siddharth’s place? Any news about a new apartment?”

“My broker is looking. Siddharth is seriously cool. We ordered dinner online tonight also. I offered to cook, but he wouldn’t listen.”

“Yeah, that’s what he’s like. A total glutton for unhealthy food. That’s why he keeps getting into fights with his wife. You should meet his wife. She is very sweet.”

"She must be. But I think when you are sweet, everything around you seem sweet," Vihaan said quietly, not sure how Tisha would take the compliment.

But Tisha didn't seem to mind for she laughed a little. "Or maybe when we are foolish, everything seems sweet." There was a sudden, unexpected bitterness in her voice. Vihaan noticed that and grew contrite. "Hey, Tisha, why are you talking like that? Is everything alright?"

"Sure. I'm always cool. I'll see you tomorrow then. I just wanted to check on you," Tisha said hastily, trying to be evasive.

"Okay. Good night then." Vihaan felt his mood dip again.

"Bye." The call disconnected.

Vihaan went back to the couch and lay down. He was restless again. He knew it in his gut that Tisha was going through some trouble even though she was pretending to be normal. He wished he could talk to her about it. But he didn't know if he had the right to broach the subject with her directly.

The next morning in the office, Vihaan saw Tisha arrive late again. She looked harassed as she settled down for work. She was so busy that she did not even get time to greet Vihaan once. Midway through the day, Vihaan saw her walking out with Rehan. They were deep in a serious discussion as they walked out, with eyes for no one and nothing else. His heart sank. After that Vihaan and his team were called for a meeting with the project manager and he didn't get to see whether Tisha came back from wherever she had gone out with Rehan.

It was during the lunch hour when Vihaan was standing at the *sutta* point outside the office complex and smoking leisurely that he saw some members of Tisha's team arrive there. Again, he wondered what Tisha was doing. He wondered if he should text her once. But right then he heard Tisha's teammates mention her name. He was instantly intrigued. He wanted to know what was being said about her. On the pretext of throwing his half-burnt cigarette in the trash can, he moved closer to them.

Prerna was saying, "Of course, Rehan is fighting with Tisha. She told me last night. She sounded really hurt over the phone. He's plain jealous of her for getting ahead in her career. That's why he's being such a jerk and hurting her. I don't understand what does she even see in him."

Kabir replied, "Try telling this to Tisha, and she'll come biting at you. She loves Rehan blindly."

Vihaan was taken aback to hear these facts against Tisha. So, his hunch that Tisha was going through some trouble was right. He could not imagine how anyone could mistreat a nice girl like Tisha. He had always thought Rehan was an amiable guy, but the truth was something else entirely. But then as he had learned over the years, girls had a knack of choosing exactly the guy who was unhealthy for them. Tisha also seemed to suffer from the same malediction.

Tisha's teammates went away soon after that, but Vihaan hung back, continuing to smoke. The sky was grey and cloudy–depressive, just like his mood.

Suddenly he heard Tisha's voice behind him. "Vihaan?"

Vihaan whipped around, surprised. Tisha looked angry and Vihaan's heart sank even further.

"What have you been telling people about us?" Tisha demanded.

Vihaan was flummoxed. "Nothing."

"Don't act innocent. Rehan heard your teammates talking about us. He was grilling me about it."

All of Vihaan's apprehensions were coming true. "I just told them that you helped me get a temporary place to stay," Vihaan defended himself. "That's all. You can come and ask Sourav and Aanchal and Mohit. They'll tell you."

Tisha glared at him with narrowed eyes for a moment, while Vihaan stood blankly. "Whatever. Listen, stay away from me, okay? I don't want Rehan to misunderstand me. We are..." Tisha dithered and then changed track at the last moment. "Never mind. You are a nice guy, I know that. But Rehan is very possessive about me, and I don't want to disrespect him." With that Tisha turned around to stride away, leaving Vihaan standing alone under the gloomy sky.

Vihaan wished once again that Tisha could be his girlfriend, that she could care for his feelings like she cared for Rehan. He sighed deeply and resumed smoking.

Part III

December, 2016

Vihaan had had a break up from his long-term girlfriend just after his college had ended in 2014. For the following two months he had been cranky, lashing out at people on the slightest provocation and keeping himself aloof from everyone around him. Only after he had started working, had he slowly come out of that negative zone. Vihaan had taken that to be normal behavior. Feeling pain for someone with whom you have spent practically all your waking hours was acceptable. And, after all, he had held himself responsible for the breakup. He used to flirt with other girls behind his girlfriend's back, so it was obvious she had to dump him when she found out. Karma, he called it inside his head.

But he didn't know why he was feeling so restless after he fell out with Tisha because of Rehan the other day.

It was almost two months since they had a proper conversation. Now all they did was exchange formal pleasantries if they ever bumped into one another in the presence of other people.

In the meantime, he had shifted to a new two-BHK apartment in Mulund. The landlord seemed like a nice person who didn't get in his way too much. So, things were going fine on that front. But now there was a pang of guilt inside him. He couldn't make peace with the knowledge that Tisha was upset with him. He saw her in the office every day, and he noticed that she smiled a lot less, talked a lot less, and looked harassed. He kept his eyes on Rehan also, but he found no signs of stress in him. Things didn't add up in Vihaan's head. He was curious but was afraid to pry into the matter.

In all the tension, he had lost his focus on music also. He had told his music teacher not to come down to his place for the time being. He would just sit with his guitar after dinner and play a little bit for himself. After he had moved out of Siddharth's place, Siddharth had tried to keep in touch with him, but soon got dissuaded by Vihaan's coldness.

One morning, Vihaan was smoking outside the office, and he saw Tisha and Rehan standing close to each other and whispering excitedly. He threw his half-burnt cigarette and strode away, unable to bear the sight. He ended up taking out his frustration on his manager's alleged new girlfriend–Sonam, a girl who had just joined his team–when she bungled up the basic team tasks that were assigned to her and failed to answer his questions in her reverse knowledge transfer. The girl was on the verge of tears by the time he was done with her. He sat fuming as Mohit whispered to him ominously, "You shouldn't have done this, dude. This might have repercussions." Mohit pointed at their team manager who was sitting on the other side of the aisle. Vihaan couldn't care less at the moment.

That night before going to bed, he logged on to his blog and deleted the poem he had written for Tisha.

Three days later, there was another team meeting. At the end of it, Vihaan was discussing work with one of the managers from another team while Tisha was hovering nearby. Vihaan learned from this guy that his promotion was being held up by his team manager. His heart sank. Immediately, Mohit's warning jumped into his mind. Feeling low, Vihaan started walking back towards his work station. And, it was then that he heard Tisha's voice. She was in front of him, talking to Prerna. Tisha was saying quite audibly, "This place is going to the dogs. Just because Vihaan scolded his junior, his promotion is being held up. How ridiculous is this!"

Prerna replied, "Do you know who that junior is? Vihaan should have known when to keep his mouth shut."

Tisha huffed, "This is what happens when we don't protest. The criterion for promotion should be a good performance, not flattering your manager's girlfriend. And, everyone knows Vihaan is good, otherwise he wouldn't have been chosen for the client site."

Suddenly, Vihaan felt a spring in his step. So, Tisha didn't have any grudges against him. Whatever might have been wrong with her, at least she didn't dislike him. He wanted to go and talk to Tisha immediately, but he controlled himself and kept walking behind them, without giving the slightest indication that he had heard her conversation with Prerna.

For the next few days, Vihaan followed Tisha's activities like a hawk, but she didn't show any signs of being interested in him. His sudden joy started subsiding again.

One evening, he walked into the Break Out Area and his eyes immediately fell on Tisha. She was sitting alone, cradling a cup of coffee between her fingers, looking lost. Vihaan was rooted to the spot. He wanted to go and talk to her but didn't know if he should. Suddenly, Tisha got up and started walking out. In the heat of the moment, Vihaan called out to her. Tisha stopped and looked around at him in surprise. Vihaan made his way towards her slowly. They stood in front of each other for a moment, looking into each other's eyes silently.

Vihaan broke the silence. "Hey, how are you?"

Tisha was at a loss for words this time around. "Fine... I'm fine." She smiled at him and walked away without another word. Vihaan was left feeling worse than ever.

He was getting ready for bed that night. He hadn't stopped thinking about Tisha for even a minute since evening. His phone rang when he was fluffing his pillow. He picked it up from the side table to check who was calling him so late and almost dropped it in shock. It was Tisha's call. He wondered if Rehan had seen them talking again and grilled her about it. Feeling terrified, he received the call. "Hello?" Vihaan squeaked.

"Hey, did I disturb you?" Tisha also sounded nervous.

"No, not at all," Vihaan said hurriedly.

There was silence from Tisha's end for a beat. "I'm sorry, Vihaan. I shouldn't have been rude to you." Her voice was low.

Vihaan's heart melted. "Listen, Tisha, I'm not mad at you."

Tisha scoffed, "You are just saying that. I know I was rude to you this morning."

"No, I understand why you lost your head that day," Vihaan protested.

"No, you don't understand. How can you? You don't know anything about me."

"Then tell me. I'd like to know you," Vihaan said recklessly.

Again, Tisha was silent. "Okay, but don't judge me."

Vihaan said sincerely, "I promise, Tisha. I'll try to understand things from your point of view."

"Okay. But we can't talk in the office. And, it's such a long story."

His heart beating fast, Vihaan let the words out, "Can we go out for dinner tomorrow? Then you can tell me everything. Actually, I have been worried for you. I see you every day and I can tell that you are not fine."

"Fine. Where do you want to go?" Tisha replied without any hesitation this time.

"Pizza Express in Powai," Vihaan suggested, "if you want. It's close to our office, and it's a nice place."

"That's settled then," Tisha said. "And, another thing. Why did you delete that poem from your blog? It was nice."

Vihaan was taken aback. "You follow my blog?"

"Yeah," Tisha replied in a brightened voice now. "I feel better when I read your poems. I've been reading your blog a lot these days."

Vihaan was amazed. "But you never commented on anything."

"You want me to?"

"Of course. It'd mean a lot to me."

"Okay. I'll do it right away then," Tisha promised. "See you tomorrow in the office, Mr. Kumar."

"Good night. I'll be waiting for your comments."

"You'll be getting them soon enough. Bye." With that Tisha disconnected the call.

Vihaan waited with bated breath to see if Tisha would really keep her words. He was still having difficulty in believing the whole thing. They hadn't talked for months and now they were going out on a date. Vihaan's thoughts halted at that word–date. It was a date for him. He wondered what Tisha would see it as. Keeping true to her words, within ten minutes Tisha commented on most of the poems he had written in the last two years. With a big smile on his face, Vihaan thanked her through a text message and went to sleep.

The next day in office, they kept their distance, pretending to be strangers. Vihaan saw Tisha with Rehan on quite a few occasions, but it didn't hit him as hard as it generally did. He was taking Tisha out on dinner, that thought sustained him throughout the day.

After the office hours, they met up in front of the auto stand like last time and took an Ola cab since Tisha's scooty was at the service center. The radio was on inside the cab and the song Dekha Hazaron Dafa Apko was playing. The mushy songs made Vihaan glance at Tisha every so often out of the corner of his eye. But Tisha seemed to be lost in her own world as she looked out of the window.

In half-an-hour, they were sitting at a cozy table in a corner of the quaint little place. When the waiter came to take their orders, Vihaan ordered spaghetti pasta with tomato gravy even before she could open the menu card. Tisha stared at him in awe. "How did you know I was going to order this?"

Vihaan smiled shyly. "I've seen you eat this at the cafeteria quite often.

Tisha's eyes grew big with surprise. She handed back the menu card to the waiter without another word. Vihaan ordered a pint of Budweiser and Corona, and the waiter went away, leaving them alone.

"I never knew you were stalking me," Tisha said, not sounding very disturbed.

"Stalking?" Vihaan was taken aback. "I wasn't stalking... it was just...you know...I noticed..."

Tisha leaned back in her chair. "Yeah, yeah I know. It's more than I can say for my boyfriend."

"You mean Rehan?" Vihaan prodded, not knowing how much curiosity he should really show in her personal life.

"Yeah, him." Tisha sighed. "He is just so careless. We have been together for two years now. And still, he can't think about anything except himself. And, look at you. We hardly know each other, and you still noticed what I like to eat."

Vihaan sat silently, again at a loss for a proper response.

Tisha took his silence as an invitation to continue. "You know I'm twenty-seven, and my parents want me to get married by the end of this year. I explained my family situation to Rehan. But he wants to do his MBA and he's just not ready for marriage right now."

"He can do his MBA after your wedding also. You can earn and he can study," Vihaan suggested.

"He wouldn't listen to any of it. Says he would get distracted if we got married right now," Tisha explained. "I don't know how to convince him. As it is, he is a Bihari, and my father is strictly against inter-caste marriage. But somehow, I'm trying to convince them about Rehan. But now he is only being careless about this."

"You should have settled everything with Rehan before talking to your family."

"I know. But when my parents started looking for grooms, I panicked and told them everything. Rehan refused to even talk to them once over the phone."

Vihaan was outraged. "That's....just..."

"Sick. Yeah, I know," Tisha said. "He has no consideration for my situation. He is just focused on his own life like a selfish prick. I keep doing things to make him happy, but my happiness doesn't matter to him at all."

There was a moment of silence. Tisha started playing with the tissue papers, lost in her thoughts, and Vihaan sat studying her beautiful face. She was looking prettier than usual. Vihaan felt Tisha had dressed up more than usual for the dinner–a fancier earring, fancier clothes, flawless makeup–but he couldn't be sure if she had made the effort for him. Meanwhile, their food was served, and they started eating.

A question rose inside him suddenly. "Does Rehan know we have come out together? Won't he mind?"

Tisha sighed again. "I don't know what he will mind and what he won't. But I didn't tell him that I have come out with you."

Vihaan didn't like this, but he let it pass. "So, what did Rehan say about us last day?"

"Are you still upset about that?" Tisha fixed him with a penetrating gaze.

Vihaan felt his thoughts get muddled up as he looked straight into her eyes. He wasn't even aware of what he was saying to her. "No, but I don't want anyone to put you in unnecessary trouble."

Tisha looked surprised. Vihaan could see that in her eyes. "Rehan thinks he is giving me my space, and in return, I should let him do whatever he chooses."

"Oh, I thought he was accusing you..." Vihaan was confused.

"No, he was not accusing. Prerna thinks he is jealous of me and that's why he's acting so detached. Just to hurt me. This is his way of pinching me."

"Why should he be jealous of you? You both work at the same level."

"Prerna thinks it's because I got chosen for the client site over him. Though our problems have been going on for much longer."

"That's petty," Vihaan said sympathetically.

"Prerna thinks I'm being foolish by staying with Rehan. She thinks I should dump him," Tisha said sadly.

Vihaan's heart thudded–in hope; in fear. "And, what do you want?"

Tisha looked at Vihaan with her big, pointed eyes. "I can't live without him." Her eyes filled with tears and Vihaan's heart sank again.

Vihaan didn't fancy his food too much after that. For the rest of the dinner, Tisha kept asking Vihaan about his life, and he answered her only half-heartedly. About an hour later they left, and Vihaan dropped her home in a cab. And, again on the way back, there were those romantic songs playing on the radio. Vihaan wondered if God was playing games just to tease him. He knew this could turn unhealthy for him, and yet he enjoyed the songs while stealing glances at her every now and then. Sometimes, his eyes would meet Tisha's and they would smile at each other and look away hastily.

The next day in office Vihaan was very busy with his work, and he didn't get much chance to check what Tisha was doing. He caught up with Maroof at the Break Out Area at noon. Maroof was leaving for London in a week, and they got into an exciting discussion about this. And it was then that he learned from Maroof that due to some internal issues Tisha's client site was being deferred for the time being. Vihaan was flabbergasted. Maroof also told Vihaan how upset Tisha was over the news.

Vihaan quickly went up to check on Tisha, but he found her huddled with Rehan at his workstation. Quietly, he went back to his desk and slumped down sadly. That night Vihaan wanted to stay back at the office a little longer to finish the remaining work. But he saw Tisha leaving without Rehan, and forgot all about his work and followed her out. He caught up with Tisha in the lift lobby.

"Hey, Tisha, wait," Vihaan called out to her.

Tisha was already inside the elevator. She held the door and allowed Vihaan to enter. They smiled at each other as the doors slid closed. But Vihaan could see the gloom in her eyes, and he decided not to bring up the topic of London.

"Would you like to go out with me tonight? I don't feel like going home."

Tisha was unsure for a moment. "I don't know, Vihaan...I..."

"Oh, come on," Vihaan insisted. "We won't stay out for too long. I'm getting bored with my work-to-home routine. Come on."

Finally, Tisha gave in and they took a cab to the Phoenix Mall. Vihaan was determined not to discuss anything depressing with her that night. Instead, he spent the time asking her about her favorite things and her childhood days. She brightened up a lot as she spoke about her life and her family. She had a younger sister who was her best friend. Vihaan was happy to see her unwind in his presence. They did a lot of window shopping and

Vihaan realized that she had a knack for buying cosmetics. Tisha kept on explaining about different brands and their subtleties–which was gluten-free and which was best for her skin. Vihaan tuned out after a point but kept nodding just to keep Tisha happy. While passing by the multiplex, they saw that Avengers was playing in the theatre that month. Vihaan immediately made a plan to watch it with Tisha over the weekend, and she agreed happily.

Soon, they made their way towards the food court. It was very crowded that night. Tisha didn't want to eat anything, so Vihaan went to get cold coffee for her and chamomile tea for himself, while Tisha went to find a table. Once they were settled down, their conversation moved on to the office politics they had to face on a daily basis and they started gossiping about their managers. Tisha told him that her onsite had been postponed and then she didn't hesitate to discuss all the people who she thought could have been behind her postponed client site trip. Vihaan was happy that at least she was talking freely and not sitting at home alone to wallow in self-pity.

Vihaan was surprised when Tisha said suddenly, "Can I have a sip?" She pointed at his tea.

Vihaan offered her his tea and she didn't hesitate to take a few sips from it. In return, she offered him her cup of coffee, but Vihaan politely refused it since he had sensitive teeth. But the pleasantness of the evening didn't last for too long. Tisha's mother called suddenly and when she told him she was out; her mother wanted to know if she was with Rehan. Tisha didn't mention Vihaan and disconnected the call soon. But her mood had dipped again. Now, their conversation veered towards Rehan.

"Rehan thinks it was a good thing that my onsite got postponed. He thinks I won't be able to manage things on my own," Tisha informed Vihaan.

The more Vihaan heard about Rehan, the more he disliked him. "And, what do you think?"

"I can take care of myself, no matter where I stay," Tisha said confidently.

Vihaan leaned towards her across the table and smiled encouragingly at her. "That's the spirit!"

Tisha also gave him a small smile, but it didn't come from the heart. "I asked him to stay with me tonight, but he refused. He said he had to study. He didn't even realize that I needed him." Vihaan kept quiet. But she started telling Vihaan all about her relationship with Rehan, and by the end of it, she was almost on the verge of tears. Vihaan sat helplessly, trying to calm her down with false hopes, knowing fully well that he wasn't doing much good. But what lifted Vihaan's mood was when Tisha said, "I think Prerna is right. I will have to leave Rehan eventually. This can't continue if he keeps treating me so badly."

Later that night, Vihaan came to drop her home in a cab again. As he watched her go inside, his self-control snapped. He wanted to be with Tisha for a few more hours. He called out to her without thinking about what he was going to say, "Tisha."

Tisha turned around to look at him. "Yes?"

Vihaan walked up to her. "Would you mind spending a little more time with me tonight?" he said, looking directly into her eyes.

Tisha was taken aback and she stayed silent for a moment. "Okay, but where do you want to go now? It's almost ten and the shops will all be closed," she said.

Vihaan smiled. "We can go for a walk, or if you don't mind, we can go up to your place?"

Tisha nodded in acquiescence and Vihaan's heart leaped in joy.

Tisha gave him a tour of her small and cozy house. It was maintained very well. Everything was in its proper place. What caught Vihaan's eyes were Tisha's framed pictures that were kept all over the house. There were small, fluffy pillows arranged neatly on the floor over a mattress near the balcony. They settled down there with steaming cups of coffee that Tisha had made and sat looking at the starry sky stretched over them, just enjoying the silence for a bit.

Tisha broke the silence this time. "Can I ask you something?"

Vihaan rolled his eyes at her. "Go ahead."

"Don't you have a girlfriend? Won't she mind that you are spending so much time with me?"

"No worries on that front. I'm single," Vihaan declared happily.

Tisha smiled at him again. "Good for you." Vihaan felt at peace with the world as he looked into her eyes. Something seemed to loosen inside Tisha and she lay down, putting her hands behind her head. Vihaan also followed suit and they lay beside each other, gazing at the starry sky.

"It's good to have you in my life, you know," Vihaan said.

"Why?" Tisha asked.

"You are a nice person. Easy to talk to and our tuning is just about right. And, you are definitely helpful," Vihaan said confidently.

"That's all?" Tisha looked at Vihaan.

Vihaan's heart skipped a beat as his eyes got jerked towards her. He hesitated for a moment and then plunged on, "You are very beautiful."

Tisha didn't take her eyes off Vihaan. "Thanks," she mumbled.

Vihaan asked, "Do you like me?"

"Of course," Tisha said nonchalantly. "You are a nice guy."

"How do you know that?"

Tisha had the answer ready. "I heard everyone praise you in the office. I saw you control yourself when your manager canceled your promotion."

Vihaan nodded.

"I knew from all that you are a nice person. And, I felt it myself also since we started talking, and you present your views without being judgmental; I mean a lot of people don't do that."

Vihaan stayed silent. The night was panning out in a way he could never have imagined.

"I was relieved when I heard you'd be coming with me to London," Tisha revealed. "But I don't know whether

I'll really get to go there," Tisha's voice got sad again and she got up to sit with her hands around her knees.

Vihaan also sat up and stared at Tisha's sad face for a moment. Blurring his line, he placed a hand on her arm just to comfort her. "Don't worry. Things will work out for you," he said softly.

Tisha turned her big eyes on Vihaan and fixed him with a penetrating gaze. "Am I not good enough for Rehan?" Her eyes filled with tears.

"Hey, don't think like that. Rehan has no idea what he has. He is a fool not to realize it. It's not your fault."

"You are just saying that to make me feel better," Tisha protested in a choked voice.

"No!"

Tisha stared at him silently for a bit and then looked away, wiping her tears away. She seemed to get cold and pulled in her knees tighter. The silence stretched. Vihaan was feeling blank. He had no idea what he could say or do to make Tisha feel any better. So, he sat thinking about Rehan's good fortune again.

It was a complete shock for Vihaan when Tisha rested her head on his shoulder all of a sudden. Vihaan felt everything inside him freeze–in fear, in excitement–he couldn't name the exact emotion.

"You mind?" Tisha asked.

"No," Vihaan mumbled. He sounded like he had a bad cold.

"Thanks for giving me company tonight."

"It's nice being with you." Vihaan's head had stopped working by then, and he went ahead with his instincts. Silently, he put his arms around Tisha. "I'll be there whenever you need me."

Without any notice, Tisha straightened up and placed a quick peck on Vihaan's cheek. "Thanks."

Vihaan stared at her, gobsmacked. Tisha gave him a small smile and was about to get up. But Vihaan grabbed her hand and pulled her back. "Honestly, Tisha, I," he mumbled and then after a beat he continued, "I like you."

Tisha stared back at him with unblinking eyes. "What do you want from me?"

"I don't want anything from you," Vihaan breathed in a husky voice. "I just want you."

"I don't know what to say," Tisha's voice was becoming smaller by the minute.

Vihaan moved ahead recklessly and kissed her on the lips. Then he looked into her eyes again, his heart thudding frantically. Vihaan tucked her hair behind her ear and Tisha looked down shyly.

Instead of moving back or pushing him away, Tisha leaned in closer to Vihaan and he took the opportunity to put his arms around her and hold her close. Tisha hid her face in his chest for a moment and then looked up to stare into his eyes.

Vihaan lowered his face again to kiss her. And, this time Tisha responded. And, slowly the moment built up so they lost track of reality and got lost into the sensations, into each other. Vihaan kissed her as he would never get to see her again and Tisha responded like she was on fire.

It was a long while before they broke the kiss. Vihaan kept his arms wrapped around her and they stayed like that for a while till Tisha started crying suddenly. "I don't want to cheat on Rehan."

Vihaan's heart sank and he felt blank again—a blankness that was filled with cold dread. "This doesn't have to mean anything if you don't want it to," he managed to say, wiping her tears away gently.

Tisha drew back from Vihaan and looked him in the eye. "You won't judge me for this?" she demanded to know.

"Of course not," Vihaan promised her. "We will always be friends," Vihaan said not knowing how he would make this happen because his heart was breaking into pieces.

Just then Rehan called on Tisha's mobile. Vihaan somehow managed to hold back his tears. "I should leave."

He got up and walked away as Tisha sat watching helplessly.

Part IV

Vihaan's eyes were itching with tiredness when he went to the office the next day since he had not slept all night. He kept glancing at Tisha's way and noticed that she also looked down. He kept wondering if he could ask her to go out with him for a few minutes and discuss what happened last night. But he could not gather up the courage to do so. He was absolutely certain that she would reject him, and if he tried to be too pushy, she might even ask him to stay away from her. But it was becoming harder by the minute to control the anxiety inside him, and he could hardly focus on work all day.

It was sometime before lunch when he gave up on badgering his brain to focus, and made his way to the

Break Out Area. Mohit also accompanied him. They were drinking coffee when Vihaan's eyes fell on Tisha. She had also arrived with Prerna and Kabir. Their eyes met and Vihaan's heart started racing. He was in a dilemma again; Should he talk to her or not? It was Tisha who silently showed him the way. Not before long, he saw Tisha's colleagues walk away once they had finished their coffees, while Tisha stayed back. She took a seat in a far corner of the room and looked at him pointedly. Then she started playing with her phone, seemingly oblivious of Vihaan's presence.

Mohit dumped his empty cup coffee in the trash can and came back to Vihaan. "Come on, let's go."

Vihaan had already finished; he had just been waiting for Mohit. "I need to go to the washroom. I'll catch up with you later," Vihaan said casually.

Mohit nodded and left.

Drawing in a deep breath, Vihaan walked up to Tisha's table, "Hi," he said, trying to appear confident, though his insides were nervous as hell. "May I sit with you?"

Tisha looked up at him and nodded silently. Her face didn't betray any emotion and Vihaan couldn't be sure as to what she was thinking. Vihaan took a seat across from her. Both of them seemed to be out of words, and just to make up for the awkwardness, Vihaan forced himself to speak. "How are you now?"

"Fine." Tisha's voice was small.

"Good...that's good." Vihaan lost heart then and tried to get up.

Tisha spoke up hastily, "I took a decision last night."

Vihaan still had his eyes on her. He sat down and asked with apprehension, "What decision?" His heart was thudding again.

"I should break up with Rehan. We...It would be better for the both of us," Tisha announced with uncertainty, looking straight at Vihaan.

A thrill ran up Vihaan's spine as he sat silently, looking for the correct words. Primarily there was only one thing that he absolutely needed to know right now that whether they could be together. But the words and the emotions got all jumbled up inside him. All he managed to say was, "So, what are you going to do now?"

"I have to tell my parents about this first. Then, I need to focus on my work also. I really want to go to the client site."

Tisha's plans were fair enough, but Vihaan couldn't see where he fit into the picture. And, yet, here she was, discussing the matter with him. He wondered if he should just say the thing that he wanted to say. But his tongue wouldn't work, the words wouldn't form on his lips.

"We should get back to work now," Tisha said in the same low voice.

Vihaan nodded and they got up together. They went back to their work stations together but didn't say another word to each other, each stuck in their own turmoil. They went back to work and tried to focus, but by coincidence or by some destined design, their eyes kept meeting every now and then for the rest of the day, as if they were getting tied together in some intangible way. Each time that happened they smiled at each other and Vihaan felt his heart race.

That night as he lay on his bed, sleep evaded him. He kept tossing and turning in his bed restlessly. It was becoming impossible for him to decide on his own and he felt a strong urge to discuss the matter with his teammates since they were the closest friends he had in Mumbai. But then again, he remembered how word had spread the last time he had talked to them about Tisha. He didn't want to create any rumors in the office. It wouldn't be good for either of their careers or for their reputation. As these disturbing thoughts kept going around in his head, slowly he started falling asleep. He had just dozed off when his phone rang. He was up in an instant, his heart pumping hard as if it was some internal siren. And, when he saw it was actually Tisha's call, he sat bolt upright and received it.

"Hi," Tisha breathed into the phone.

"Hey," Vihaan was again at a loss for words.

"Did I disturb?"

"No," Vihaan said hastily.

"Can I ask you something?" Tisha asked.

"Sure."

"That poem you wrote last day on your blog. Was that for me?"

Vihaan's heart stopped for a moment. His moment of truth had come, and without any thought, he blurted out, "Yeah, it was, actually." There was a moment of silence. "I like you, Tisha. If you are not comfortable this doesn't have to mean anything. We can continue the way we are. I don't want to pressurize you in any way. I just..."

"I know how you feel about me, Vihaan," Tisha cut him short. "But I'm so messed up right now and it's really difficult for me to make clear decisions about the future."

"I understand that." Vihaan fell silent again. "Please take your time. I just want you to be happy."

"You have been so kind and patient with me throughout this mess. I'm glad we became friends." There was no hesitation in Tisha's voice as she confessed her feelings.

Vihaan felt like his heart would jump out of his mouth. "I wish we could be together right now."

Tisha mumbled, "We are meeting in the office tomorrow." There was hope in her voice, a hope that Vihaan couldn't stop from seeping deep into his heart."

Vihaan felt really bad for Tisha then. "So, when are you going to tell Rehan?"

"Actually, Vihaan. I don't want to do this in a hurry," Tisha's voice was low again. She sounded nervous.

"What does that mean?" Vihaan's eyebrows puckered in confusion, all his soaring joy crashing to the ground in one second.

"Rehan is going to sit for his CAT exams in December. He's preparing very hard for it right now. If I break up with him, it'll distract him. I don't want to be so mean. He might not know his responsibilities. But as a friend, as a well-wisher I can't be so selfish," Tisha explained.

Vihaan fell in love with Tisha a little more at that point. "Of course. You are right."

"Thanks," Tisha gushed happily. "So, are we still going to that movie this weekend?"

"Definitely. The treat is on me," Vihaan promised. "Thanks, Tisha. I mean, I never thought we could be together. This feels surreal right now."

"Yeah. Even I never thought I'd find someone like you someday. It's like finding the right person at the wrong time."

And, on they continued for the next hour or so. That was how their late-night phone calls started. Vihaan's teammates could hardly fail to notice the joy radiating from him in the following days. But he didn't say anything to them. Whenever he was asked awkward questions, he deflected them by giving excuses for his client site stint. Thus, Vihaan and Tisha continued with their cordial behavior in the office premises, never letting anybody guess the truth.

Vihaan had never been happier. Tisha called him every morning to wake him up. Vihaan's day started with her voice and ended with her voice, and there was nothing more he could ask for then. She shared every little thing with him through text messages, and Vihaan also started sharing all his thoughts with her. Vihaan started writing more and more poetry, and he wanted to make Tisha a part of his creative self, and he intentionally made grammatical mistakes in his lines. He would show them to Tisha before posting them on his blog. When she pointed out the mistakes and corrected them for him, Vihaan felt a warmth of security envelope his heart, as if he had made the ultimate decision of his life, though he never told this to Tisha.

But their days of being together was numbered because 31st December was fast approaching, and he had to leave for London. There was a lot of packing to be done and a lot of formalities to be covered in the office. Vihaan was being forced to spend a lot of time on these practicalities and it irked him very much because it was taking away from his time with Tisha. But Tisha was very patient throughout this. She took it on herself to help Vihaan shop for all the warm clothes and other necessary items he would need. To Vihaan and Tisha, it seemed as if that one month has passed in the blink of an eye. And, then before they knew it, new years' eve was there.

The night before 31st, Tisha came to Vihaan's apartment to help him pack all his luggage. It took them almost the entire afternoon to gather everything in one place and pack the trolley bags he was taking with him. It was around evening when they finished all their work and slumped down on the bed side-by-side. They lay exhausted for a while, not talking, their arms touching. Vihaan wound his fingers into Tisha's and turned his face towards her. He was taken aback to see tears running down the corner of her eyes. Vihaan hastily propped himself up on his elbow and hovered over Tisha.

Vihaan asked worriedly, "What happened?" He wiped her tears away gently.

They looked into each other's eyes silently for a while, their breaths mingling together. "I wish I could also go to London with you, Vihaan."

Vihaan felt his heart twist at the sadness on her face. "We'll be together, soon." And, they hugged each other tightly after that. Vihaan drew back so that he could kiss her. But Tisha pushed him away. Vihaan looked at her quizzically.

"Can we do this after I break up with Rehan? I don't want to feel like a schmuck."

Vihaan had lost all his ability to think when he looked deep into her eyes. He just nodded his head like a puppet tied to a string.

"I have brought something for you," Tisha said, moving away from Vihaan. Vihaan didn't want to let go of her, but he didn't stop her.

Tisha got up and went outside to the drawing room to where her bag was kept on the couch. Vihaan followed. Tisha took out a wrapped package from her bag and handed it to Vihaan, encouraging him to unwrap it with a nod of her head. Vihaan ripped apart the wrappings and took out a minion keyring. His face split into a huge grin and he hugged Tisha quickly. "Thanks, Tisha ji. This is amazing."

Tisha also smiled happily. "You like Minions. So, when I saw it, it reminded me of you."

Vihaan liked his gift very much and hugged Tisha again, and they stayed together like that for a long time.

Vihaan's flight was at 1.30 a.m. on the 31st. His parents and brothers and his sister were coming to see him off. It would have been awkward if they saw Tisha at his place. So, they said their farewells soon after that before his family members could arrive. Tisha got teary again and Vihaan was in no better state. When Vihaan stood in front of the main gate and saw Tisha going away in a cab, a feeling of emptiness settled inside him. And, from that moment till he reached the airport, even with his family, all he thought about was Tisha.

Vihaan bid everyone farewell with a heavy heart. It was true, Vihaan was excited about his London stint, but as he walked away from his loved ones, all he felt was the pain of separation. When he got into the flight, he called Tisha one last time. She wished him luck and promised that the next time they met, there would be no issues between them. On that hopeful note, Vihaan disconnected the call and turned his phone on to the flight mode.

The Jet Airways flight that Vihaan was taking to Heathrow would take him to his dream city in the next nine hours. Hoping that everything remained the way it was, Vihaan gave himself up to his destiny as the flight took off into the air.

Almost nine hours later, Vihaan landed in Heathrow. He stepped out of the airport to breathe in the fresh air of London. It was almost five degrees that morning. He had to take out his jacket and put it over his sweater. As he looked around to take in his new and grander, fancier surroundings, a thrill of excitement stole over him. It was drizzling slightly, and his breathes came out in smoke. It was not the ideal weather for him, and yet at that moment, he enjoyed the scene, invigorated by the newness of everything around him. He decided to smoke, just to celebrate the beginning of his new venture. While he stood smoking, he noticed the queue of black cabs lined across the street. He boarded one to make his way towards the house that one of his colleagues had already rented for him.

Part V

Vihaan settled down in Wembley where the Gujarati and other Indian communities stayed. One of his colleagues had found a PG for him and he was sharing his room with another guy from a different company. They were amiable roomies, but could not get close to each other. For the first one month, Vihaan put all his focus into his work. He would get up on six every morning and reach the office by seven-thirty or eight. This was a different schedule from what he had followed all his life, but he was enjoying this. His colleagues were warm and helpful people who helped him fit in. The office culture was also as different as possible from India, and Vihaan really appreciated the unwavering focus with which his new colleagues worked daily. He felt really inspired by the dedication all around him and he threw himself into his work even more. Though work was fantastic for him, but beyond that it was lonely. For a lack of companionship, he didn't get the heart to explore London too much, but he was very proud of the fact that he was in London and working there. The sense of achievement he felt saw him through his acute homesickness.

Life in London was also completely different than what it was in India. Everything here was very disciplined and people led their lives by the rule book, and for a true-blue Indian like Vihaan, that was a little tough to adjust to after spending a boisterous and carefree life. The biggest hurdle he was facing was-food. He couldn't cook in the house, so he had to rely on takeaways from Indian food joints and on the office cafeteria. But since he was a vegetarian, his choice of food again got limited.

During his first month in London, he came across Maroof again. And, through his roomie, he met Amit. By some chance, Vihaan, Maroof, and Amit ended up becoming very close friends, and their companionship started taking Vihaan's mind off his isolation. Amit had been living in London for almost three years and he tutored Vihaan and Maroof about life in London. So, Amit became the go-to guide for all things in London.

And, through everything, Vihaan had Tisha with him. Vihaan returned home from office around six or seven at night. By that time, it was around seven at night in India. But Tisha stayed awake every night till two to video chat with Vihaan. Sometimes, she would even fall asleep while talking to Vihaan. After tedious days of work, seeing Tisha's smiling face was like an oasis of calm for him. True, he couldn't hold her hand anymore or play with her hair anymore, but her smile drove away all his exhaustion. They told each other everything that was happening in their lives. They often discussed Rehan's matter, and it was starting to weigh heavy on their minds again. But Tisha promised him every night that she would end it quickly. What Tisha was concerned about was Vihaan's isolated life in London. She could see that being lonely all the time was making him short-tempered and cranky again, and this disturbed her. She discussed this openly with Vihaan, but he couldn't see how he could handle this.

It was during this time that Maroof and Amit started looking for a Victorian house to rent. Victorian houses were big bungalow-type houses with three-four big rooms. When Tisha heard about this, she suggested Vihaan shift with them. Vihaan didn't like the idea at first; he had kind of gotten used to his present establishment, but Tisha convinced him about it. He talked to Maroof and Amit about this. So, whenever Maroof and Amit went looking for houses, they sent him the pictures. Soon, they found the perfect little house in Hounslow, and the three men moved in together. In the presence of his new best friends, Vihaan's mood started lifting again. Maroof took charge of the cooking which was strictly vegetarian since Amit was a Jain, and Vihaan took charge of the cleaning. Amit was the lazy one and they had to practically threaten him with starvation to send him out to do the grocery shopping. Amit also started taking them out to roam around London, and soon Vihaan fell in love with Oxford Street and Regent Street that housed famous stores inside old colonial buildings. Now, Vihaan got the chance to take out his DSLR and start with his photography. He was more interested in capturing the landscape. But since he was always surrounded by his friends, they would request him to take their pictures, and most of his time would go in clicking their pictures. He soon became very popular for his photography in his office circle. So, life was again on an upswing for Vihaan.

On Vihaan's birthday, he went to the office as usual and sat working at his desk. His birthday rolled in, but he didn't have any plans for the day. He had never been fond of celebrating his birthday and he never created a hue and cry over such supposedly special occasions. He was just happy to receive birthday greetings from the PMO team in his office. So, it was a complete surprise when he received a bouquet of flowers in the middle of the day. His colleagues in London were not very curious or nosey, so no one converged on him to ask who had sent those flowers, but he felt a thrill nonetheless. As soon as he saw those flowers, he knew it had to be Tisha because no one else could be so thoughtful. Since he was in the middle of some urgent work, he couldn't talk to her immediately, so he just pinged her to thank her and promised to talk to her once he returned home. As soon as Vihaan reached home that night, without even freshening up, he got into a video call with Tisha.

But things can never be too smooth for a long stretch. Rehan's CAT exams were long over, and it was high time for Tisha to break up with him. But she was losing her nerve and she kept postponing it. Vihaan started getting irritated and that led to fights between them. Tisha knew she was wrong, and so she took all the taunts quietly. Every time he said something unpleasant to her, he saw her face fall. Immediately he felt bad and apologized hastily. And, slowly Tisha got normal again. Vihaan tried with all his might to school his growing anxiety, and he encouraged her every night to talk to Rehan.

And, one fine day, in the last week of January, Tisha plucked up the courage and promised that she would talk to Rehan. Vihaan spent the whole day in office in a heightened state of anxiety. He couldn't settle into anything all day. But when he returned home and got on to his daily video chat, it was to receive a piece of grave news, Rehan was refusing to accept her decision. And, Tisha was looking shattered by her ordeal. Vihaan didn't like seeing her get emotional over Rehan now, but he didn't vex his frustration on her when she obviously needed his support. Vihaan suggested that she should tell Rehan about him. Tisha refused to do this since she knew that words would travel and rumors would spread. But now that they were so serious about each other, Vihaan couldn't understand why Tisha would care about rumors. But he didn't press the point. He wanted Tisha to do things at her own pace. By this point, he could do anything to keep her happy, even if it meant agreeing to things that he didn't believe in.

With things looking bleak for Tisha and his relationship, Vihaan was having a rough time again. The brief spell of happiness he had enjoyed with Maroof and Amit had evaporated, and he was avoiding them. When asked questions, he refused to give a straight answer, and slowly they were starting to avoid Vihaan whenever they saw him looking grumpy. With Tisha's reluctance to leave Rehan, Vihaan might have had doubts about Tisha's intentions had she not made him talk to her younger sister, Bali. One day, when she was staying with her in Mumbai, Tisha was on a call with Vihaan when Bali walked into the room. Bali got curious about whom she was talking to, so Tisha made her talk to Vihaan over the phone. They did not tell Bali that they were serious about each other though. Bali was a friendly, talkative girl, and Vihaan enjoyed interacting with her briefly that day. Tisha told him later that before they could talk to her parents, they would have to get Bali in their team. Vihaan's unease was appeased on hearing Tisha making plans like these for their future. After that day, Bali used to ping Vihaan sometimes, and they had short and casual chats over the phone. Bali's inclusion made Vihaan feel as if he was getting more involved in Tisha's life, and this feeling helped him stay calm through all the anxiety.

Tisha's issues with Rehan continued for almost a week, and during this time, Vihaan supported Tisha in every way he could from so far away. So, it was the biggest relief when Rehan finally accepted defeat and agreed to move on with his life. Vihaan and Tisha were ecstatic.

And, it was during this turmoil that Valentines' Day came along. Since this was their first Valentine's Day together so he wanted to make it memorable for Tisha, and he sent a bunch of carnations and fairy lights for her-things that Vihaan knew she was fond of. That day he made up his mind to take Tisha out on a vacation. But he kept this idea to himself lest things didn't pan out as planned, and then he worked out a plan for himself first. He browsed through trip planning websites and decided to take a small vacation for five days in France with Tisha. But when he told this to her, she refused. No matter how hard Vihaan tried to convince her she wouldn't budge. She was afraid of her parents finding out about Vihaan so soon because she was yet to tell them about him. Vihaan tried to promise her that they wouldn't post any pictures online and wouldn't talk to anyone about where they were going. But Tisha wouldn't change her mind for him at any cost. Bali was staying with her at that point, so she didn't know how she could go out for a vacation leaving her alone at home.

But by now, Vihaan was desperate to meet Tisha and be with her. If Tisha couldn't come to him, he had to go to him. So, he took leave approval from his manager and booked a flight ticket to India before telling Tisha anything. When everything was settled, Vihaan finally decided to inform Tisha. When Tisha got the news on a video call, her eyes shone with joy, and Vihaan knew immediately that he had done the right thing. Tisha's excited voice drew Bali's attention and she overheard their conversation. By then Vihaan and Bali had become quite friendly with each other. That night, Tisha's excitement revealed all the truth that they had been hiding from Bali. It didn't take Bali long to understand that something was going on between Vihaan and Tisha. She just smiled naughtily at the two of them and said to Vihaan, "Get me mint chocolates from London." Relieved that Bali was happy about their relationship, he agreed immediately.

So, Vihaan and Tisha spent the rest of February and the beginning of March making exciting plans for what they would do once Vihaan reached Mumbai. But since happiness can't stay unblemished by flecks of sadness, their happiness too was marred by the looming shadow of Rehan. Tisha had an inkling that her parents would be relieved to hear that she had broken up with Rehan, but still, she couldn't be sure of what they would demand of her next. When she plucked up the courage and informed them about her break-up, they accepted the whole thing calmly. They didn't show any overt emotions over the whole situation. Their silence had Tisha worried initially, but Vihaan convinced her not to bother too much about this. Slowly, as the days went by and her parents didn't mention Rehan again, Rehan started fading into the past, both for Tisha and for Vihaan.

And, finally, it was time for Vihaan to go to India. He arrived in Mumbai one fine morning in the last week of March. He called Tisha once he had got his luggage from the baggage claim. He was touched to know she had been cleaning her house all morning just to please him. She knew Vihaan liked everything to be spanking clean since he used to tease her jokingly about the mess in her kitchen sometimes.

Tisha was supposed to meet him at the airport, but she was running late and she apologized for it profusely. She asked him to meet her in front of the Starbucks store in the airport. So, he reached the spot and kept waiting for Tisha impatiently. The last few minutes of distance seemed to be the hardest to bear. And, after about forty minutes, he finally heard Tisha's bright voice behind him, "Hey, Mr. Kumar, checking out other girls in my absence, are you?"

Vihaan whipped around, and as his eyes finally fell on her, his heart soared with joy. She was looking pretty in a floral dress and red lipstick. Her eyes were shining in joy. Tisha was smiling at him happily. And, for Vihaan she was the most beautiful sight in the world, a beauty that he knew was his to cherish all his life. Unable to contain his joy, Vihaan took her in his arms and kissed her quickly. Tisha was looking shy when he let go of her. Vihaan took her hand firmly. "I missed you, Tisha."

Tisha looked into his eyes. "Yes, it's a good thing you decided to come."

Soon, they went to Tisha's place, and there Vihaan met Bali. Bali was also beautiful like Tisha, very bubbly and chirpy. She was happy to meet Vihaan in person finally. The three of them sat down together for a while once Vihaan had freshened up to catch up with each other's news. It was then that Bali expressed her disappointment with the two of them for not sharing their secret with her earlier. Vihaan apologized to her, and Tisha promised that she wouldn't hide anything from her again. Bali was appeased thus, and she lost no time in declaring that Tisha had made a better choice this time. Laughing at Bali's comments, Vihaan took out all the gifts he had brought for the ladies from London and handed them out.

Once lunch was over and Bali had gone out of the house, Tisha took him into her room and they lay together on the bed. This time Tisha did not hesitate to snuggle in his arms and when Vihaan tried to kiss her, she did not object. In fact, Vihaan felt as if she too had been waiting for the moment. And, they savored each other's touch for a long time, without anyone there to disturb them in their moment of reunion. Every pain and every turmoil they had been through for the last three months melted as they lost themselves in each other.

Later that night, Vihaan and Tisha got ready to go out and celebrate. They invited Bali to accompany them as well. But she refused to be the third wheel and wanted to stay back at home. Vihaan and Tisha convinced her to accompany them since they didn't want her to get bored at home alone. They had a blast that night as they watched a movie, and Vihaan and Tisha held hands throughout the screening. Life seemed to take on a different hue when Tisha was with him, Vihaan noticed. Movies felt more entertaining, talking felt much easier, laughter came more naturally–Vihaan fell more in love with Tisha with every passing moment.

When they came back to Tisha's place after dinner, Bali went to sleep in the smaller room. Tisha took him to the balcony again. Vihaan was pleasantly surprised to see that Tisha had hung the fairy lights he had sent her on Valentine's Day all over the balcony. Tisha turned on the fairy lights and they twinkled merrily at them. They sat down on that mattress where it had all started for them, just cuddling with each other and talking. "I'm worried about my parents' reaction," Tisha confessed.

"Why?"

"They were against Rehan because he was Bihari. And, you are Bihari as well. So, you know..." Tisha's voice trailed off.

Vihaan felt his heart sink. "We will convince them," he said, trying to stay positive. "We have already crossed so many hurdles, we can get through this also."

"I'm scared," Tisha said in a low voice.

"What are you scared of?" Bali's voice came from behind. She walked towards them and sat down on the mattress. "Mind if I join you guys? I couldn't sleep."

"No, it's okay," Vihaan said. "Your sister thinks your parents are not going to like me because of my caste."

"Oh, yeah, our parents are very orthodox when it comes to that. Their status in society is very important for them."

"Status?" Vihaan was flummoxed. "But Tisha and I... we work together in the same company. I come from a respectable family. And, I love their daughter. What possibly can they dislike about me?"

"My father is very high-headed, Vihaan. I don't know how to explain this to you," Tisha started explaining. "See, we live in a close-knit community. My father works in Steel India. Over there, everyone is competing with everyone else, and everyone is boasting about their children's achievements to each other. Bali and I always had to maintain a certain standard. There was no way we could take anything for granted and not perform well."

Vihaan was still confused. "Yes, all that's well. But how can I seem unfit to them?"

"I told you, Vihaan. You are a Bihari. We are Brahmins. If I marry outside my caste, our acquaintances will laugh behind our backs, and think that we have fallen in position. My father won't accept all that."

"Tisha...this is..." Vihaan bristled indignantly. He was feeling agitated now as he looked into Tisha's disturbed eyes.

But Bali intervened. "Tisha, honestly, I've never seen you happier. You somehow come to life when you are around Vihaan. And, Vihaan is a nice guy. Don't be so pessimistic about this."

Tisha tutted. "It's not giving me any joy, Bali, being pessimistic as you call it. I love Vihaan, too, okay? I just don't know how we will handle everything."

"I'll help, Tisha," Bali said confidently. "I promise, I'll talk to mom and dad on your behalf. I'll tell them I've met Vihaan and that he's really nice. They will have to listen. They also want us to be happy."

Vihaan was somewhat relieved and really touched. "Thanks, Bali."

Bali smiled at Vihaan. "Okay, I'll go back to the bedroom now. I should try and get some sleep. You guys want to stay here, or swap places?"

Vihaan said, "No, you go and sleep." He looked at Tisha's face. "I believe there's more to this conversation."

Once Bali was gone, Tisha put her head on his chest. "Do you promise to stay with me no matter what happens?"

Vihaan took her hand in his. "We will fight for each other till the end." Vihaan kissed her forehead tenderly, and they continued discussing the possibility of their relationship.

Vihaan spent another joyful day with Tisha and Bali and then left for Hyderabad to visit his family members. Everyone was very happy to see him after so long and so was Vihaan. Vihaan didn't tell them that he had arrived in India two days ago, and mercifully no one checked his passport, so his lie went unnoticed. But, no one failed to notice that he might be present with them but his mind was clearly elsewhere. One night, his sister-in-law caught him video chatting with Tisha. Vihaan hastily turned over the phone screen. His sister-in-law, Priyanka, looked at him pointedly. "What are you hiding, Vihaan?"

Vihaan tried to appear nonchalant. "Oh, it was just a call from the office."

"Really? Why are you blushing then?" Priyanka wouldn't relent.

"No! Blushing, what...no!" Vihaan tried to wave it off.

Priyanka smiled at him knowingly. "It's okay. We want you to be happy. Our best wishes are always with you." With that Priyanka left him alone.

Vihaan immediately got back to the call with Tisha and told her what had happened. Tisha got gloomy on hearing this. "We will convince our parents. Won't we, Vihaan?"

"Of course, Tisha. We are meant to be together, you will see," Vihaan promised with all his heart.

Soon, Vihaan's leave was over, and he flew back to London, feeling as if he was leaving himself behind with Tisha.

Part VI

April, 2017

Vihaan was getting back into his monotonous routine in London again, and somehow it felt harder this time around. Tisha's absence was disturbing him worse than before now. He tried spending more time with Maroof and Amit, but somehow, he seemed to be living for the few hours at night which he spent chatting with Tisha over the phone. He was hoping this neediness in him would dissipate with time, because it was hampering his focus on work. He had hardly explored London, but he didn't feel the curiosity anymore.

About two weeks after his return from India, Vihaan came back from another exhausting day at the office and freshened up quickly to get on a call with Tisha. As usual, her grin quietened all the restless in him, and the completely unexpected news she gave him right then made his heart leap in joy. "You are coming to London!" Vihaan exclaimed ecstatically.

Tisha nodded, equally excited. "Yes, it was confirmed today. I'll be reaching there next Sunday."

From that moment onwards, Vihaan couldn't wait for the five intervening days to pass. The hands of the clock seemed to be have become jammed as they moved ahead sluggishly. But no matter how excited he was, he was forced to school himself because Maroof and Amit didn't know anything about them, and Tisha wanted to keep it that way for now. So, it wasn't Vihaan who put forth the idea of Tisha moving in with them, but Maroof, because Maroof and Tisha being from the same team were very close friends. But Vihaan agreed readily when Maroof suggested that they invite Tisha to join them. Tisha also agreed when Maroof told her about this. Vihaan didn't particularly like getting sidelined like this but at that point, he was more than happy to just sit in anticipation for Tisha's arrival.

With Tisha about to join them, their living arrangements inside the house had to be changed. So, Maroof and Amit moved into the first-floor room, while Tisha and Vihaan were allocated separate rooms of their own on the ground floor. Vihaan didn't tell anyone, but he was secretly relieved to have been allotted the room closer to Tisha's. He didn't have the chance to do anything extravagant to welcome Tisha, so instead, he put all his efforts in cleaning the house.

Every night when he went to sleep after talking to Tisha, he felt as if all his dreams were coming true at once–he was working in London, he was earning loads, he had a fabulous girlfriend who he loved with all his heart, and she was now coming to live with him. He couldn't imagine anything else he might need right then to be happy and content. Just a few days back he had been dreading his year away from Tisha, and now he was wishing for this year to last forever.

Vihaan woke up early on Sunday, unable to settle down on anything. He made tea for everyone and got ready. Tisha's flight was landing around eleven, and Maroof was supposed to go and pick her up. He forced Maroof and Amit to wake up earlier than was usual for them on Sundays. Grumbling at him, Amit had his breakfast and went to the gym. Maroof went to get ready, while Vihaan sat twiddling his thumbs impatiently. When Maroof was about to set off from the house, Vihaan couldn't hold himself back any longer. "You mind if I come with you to the airport? I'm getting bored at home."

Maroof didn't catch the anxious undertone in Vihaan's would-be casual voice, "The more the merrier," he said.

Vihaan grinned to himself as he hastened to join Maroof.

About two hours later, when Vihaan's eyes finally fell on Tisha, he wanted to run to her and kiss her, but all he could do in front of everyone was give her a polite one-armed hug like an acquaintance. Somehow, in these few days, Tisha seemed to have become more beautiful for Vihaan. While they took a cab back home, he sat listening to her chirpy voice as she chatted non-stop with Maroof. Their eyes met every so often and they grinned at each other shyly. It was a sunny day, coincidentally, quite contrary to the normal weather conditions in London, and for Vihaan it was turning out to be one of the most memorable days of his life.

Tisha liked their house and her room. She met Amit and they instantly hit it off. She insisted on helping them make lunch, and they sat together to eat, chatting about Tisha's sudden client site stint. She told them all the news back at their office in India. They found the most inconsequential things to talk about, and they laughed at apparently the silliest jokes. The usual sombre mood inside their house had suddenly been brightened up by Tisha's hearty laughter and her carefree chatter. Vihaan fell in love with her anew that day.

It was quite late when Vihaan went to bed. He had hardly got two minutes alone with Tisha all day, and he was rankled by this. So, when Tisha came into his room after everyone else had retired to their rooms, he couldn't stop himself from taking her in his arms and kissing her passionately. They sat together for a long time that night, just chatting and stealing kisses every now and then, without bothering about the fact that the next day they had to go to the office early.

When Tisha joined office, Vihaan and Maroof helped her settle in. And, outside the office, life became exciting. Tisha took over the cooking duties now, and Vihaan gladly agreed to help her with it. Vihaan found joy in packing her lunch for office and making tea for her if she was taking longer in the shower. Being an early bird, Vihaan woke Tisha up with bed tea on weekends because she never liked rising early in the morning. Tisha grumbled initially at being woken up, but when Vihaan's face fell, she perked him up again with sweet kisses. Slowly, every moment in

Vihaan's life was starting to revolve around Tisha, and Tisha was finding joy in getting closer to him with every passing day.

It wasn't just Vihaan's life that Tisha was touching. She was turning the three men in the house from housemates to close friends. Earlier, the men would come back from office and retire to their rooms after dinner, but now Tisha started egging them on to go outside. Slowly, enthused by Tisha's excitement, Vihaan, Maroof, and Amit started coming out of their stupor, and every weekend they started going out to roam around London. They visited Central London, Trafalgar Square, Regent Street, Oxford Street, and whatnot. Mostly, they liked visiting the casinos. They never went overboard while gambling at the casinos but limited their expenditure limit to fifty pounds at most, and on most days, they would manage to win handsome amounts.

It was another novel experience for them when they went to visit Soho, the red-light area in London. Till that day, they had never even heard of the Gay Pride Movement. But there they saw hordes of enthusiastic gay men taking on the roads, holding hands, kissing openly. More than anything it was like a culture shock for them. But it did open their minds to a large and integral part of the society about which they had never thought much till then. Amit dragged them to a sex toy shop next. It was a curious little place, and they had fun exploring the various items on sale there. Since Amit was the most enthusiastic about this so they pulled his leg a lot.

Vihaan and Tisha liked traveling to the office together. They also left the office together every day. And, on most days they were joined by Maroof. Even if Vihaan finished work before Tisha, he would wait for her and leave with her only when she was done. It was during one such train journey to the office that they got late. Tisha's teammate called from the office to ask her where she was. Tisha was forced to lie that she was stuck in the traffic. Her teammate disconnected without saying anything after that. But Tisha started panicking. "What would they think about me, Vihaan?"

Vihaan couldn't understand why she was getting so frazzled by such a common thing. "Relax. We'll reach soon."

"Yeah, but my manager might feel I'm making excuses to go late to the office. I don't want to disappoint my new boss."

Vihaan patted her hand to calm her. "You are overthinking this now."

Tisha nodded, but she remained tensed all the way to the office, and nothing that Vihaan said could calm her down. Tisha had a bad day at work after that, and by the time they were done, she was in a really bad mood. Just to cheer her up, Vihaan suggested going shopping, just the two of them. Tisha liked the idea, and as they made their way to Oxford Street her mood started lifting slowly. Vihaan went wherever Tisha took him that night. He was a complete novice when it came to women's beauty products, and Tisha took it on herself to educate him in this sphere. She went from one shop to another browsing through cosmetics of various brands. She bought a lot of items, mostly hair care products, and taught Vihaan all the features and uses of each product. That night, Tisha shopped so extravagantly that when she came across perfumes from Victoria's Secret, Beyoncé, and Calvin Klein, she didn't get the heart to spend any more than she had already done. Vihaan noticed her sad face when she was walking away from all the things that she wanted, and right there he made up his mind to get them for her as a surprise. From there, they went to a fancy restaurant called Little Italy and ate their usual pasta with wine. By the time they returned home, Tisha was happy, and Vihaan was relieved to see her smiling again.

Their shopping trips started becoming more frequent after this, and every time Tisha left something behind, Vihaan made a mental note of it. Slowly, he started saving money to buy every item that Tisha was leaving behind in London. But he kept his plans to himself, for now, not wanting to spoil the surprise.

It was a month after Tisha's arrival in London, that the project for which she was assigned to the client site got scrapped due to funding issues. Tisha was suddenly on the brink of going back home. A gloom settled over them. Vihaan could hardly talk when Tisha gave him the news in the office cafeteria. Maroof and Amit too were shocked. Tisha lost her appetite that night, and Vihaan forced her to eat a little bit of soup for dinner. The four of them sat after dinner and decided that it would be best for Tisha to talk to her manager at the client office. But Tisha wasn't at all hopeful when she went up to discuss the matter at the office. She requested her manager to assign her to some other project at the client site. The manager did agree to consider her case, but she didn't really believe anything could happen. For the next two weeks, Vihaan started feeling suffocated whenever he thought about living without Tisha. But in the face of Tisha's depression, he had to put on a smiling face, just to keep up her morale.

It was sheer joy when Tisha's stay in London was confirmed again. They all breathed in relief and went out for a celebratory dinner that night, getting drunk without a care in the world. That night Vihaan was in Tisha's room after Maroof and Amit had gone to bed. They were lying together, holding hands, murmuring sweet nothings to each other when Tisha's phone rang. Vihaan picked up her phone from the bedside table and he was shocked to see Rehan's name flashing on the screen. Vihaan turned his eyes on Tisha questioningly. She was looking nervous as well.

Vihaan asked in a shock, "Why's he calling?"

Tisha chewed her lips nervously. "He does sometimes."

Vihaan sat bolt upright. "You never told me before!"

"It's nothing, Vihaan," Tisha defended herself. "He just accuses me of cheating on him."

Vihaan was lost for words momentarily. "Pick up the phone and see what he wants. Put it on speaker."

Tisha looked at Vihaan for a moment to gauge his reaction and received the call. Rehan didn't seem to be calling to accuse her at all. Instead, he asked her about her day and about her work. The conversation was like that between two close friends. Tisha hesitated to answer freely in front of Vihaan, but Vihaan could hear the hope in Rehan's voice. By the time the call ended, Vihaan didn't know what had struck him out of the blue.

"He is still trying to win you back, Tisha," Vihaan's voice was hoarse.

Tisha stayed silent.

"Do you realize you are giving him false hopes by encouraging him to call you like this?"

"I feel bad about whatever happened, Vihaan. If he feels a little better just talking to me then isn't it a good thing?"

"No, it isn't it!" Vihaan rounded on her. "He still wants you back. And you are making him feel he still has a chance!" Vihaan's face went hard as he fixed Tisha with a stern gaze. "Does Rehan still have a chance, Tisha? Be honest."

Tisha gaped and she retaliated, "No! It's not what you think. I'm just trying to be a friend to him. I don't want him to think anything bad of me."

"That's funny! He thinks you cheated on him. And, to be fair, you did," Vihaan said in a rough voice, trying not to be too loud, afraid that he would alert Maroof and Amit upstairs. "You didn't care then. Why do you care now? It's over between you two. Let him think whatever the hell he wants to think."

Tisha's nostrils flared angrily now. "You don't care about my image at all then? All you care about is...is your possessiveness."

They sat glaring at each other. After a minute or two, Vihaan got up and stormed out of the room. He couldn't sleep a wink that night.

The next morning there was a stiff silence between the two of them. They set out for office together and traveled together, but didn't say a word to each other. Vihaan felt his chest getting constricted with helpless anger and anxiety all day. Whenever his eyes fell on Tisha, he couldn't help remembering the bad things, and the resentment inside him seared. They returned home separately that day, and had dinner in near silence, just mumbling responses if Maroof or Amit asked them anything directly. They were thankful that the other two men were too engrossed with their own lives, and didn't notice their preoccupation.

Vihaan was surprised when he opened his bedroom door on hearing a knock and saw Tisha standing outside. He let her in without a word. Tisha entered and closed the door behind her. "I've blocked Rehan from everywhere. I won't talk to him again," Tisha announced without beating about the bush.

Vihaan stared at her for a moment, feeling a little dazed and messed up. Tisha closed the distance between them and hugged him tightly. "I never thought you'd mind if I talked to Rehan. Otherwise, I'd have been careful."

Vihaan felt all his anger seep out as he felt Tisha's heartbeat against his. "I'm sorry," Vihaan mumbled. He wound his arms around her, letting himself relax for the first time since last night.

Tisha nuzzled her face in his chest. "Can I stay here with you tonight? I couldn't sleep last night after you walked out like that."

"Me too," Vihaan confessed.

Tisha kissed him on the lips and looked into his eyes. "Don't get so worked up about everything, okay?"

Vihaan nodded, pulling her in for another kiss.

After this tiff with Tisha, Vihaan was feeling a little shaken, and he decided that they needed a break from their daily lives so that they could spend more quality time together and get to know each other better. Thus, he planned to go on foreign trips with her. He started making all the plans without telling Tisha.

One night, that weekend when Vihaan sat making travel plans in the drawing room, Tisha came up to him. "Vihaan, I have downloaded Ranjhaana from Netflix. Want to watch?"

"I've watched it already," Vihaan said without looking up from his laptop screen.

Tisha slammed his laptop screen shut without any warning, forcing Vihaan to pay her attention. She ordered, "We are going to watch it together."

Vihaan relented in the face of her strict demand. So, they sat watching the movie together on her laptop. Soon, they started getting cold, so Tisha brought a blanket and they sat under it to continue watching the movie. It was then that Maroof and Amit returned from their weekly grocery shopping and found the two of them sitting together like that. Vihaan noticed the two of them share curious glances, but Tisha remained oblivious. Instead, she asked Maroof and Amit to join them. They both had watched it earlier, but like always no one could deny Tisha anything. So, they also freshened up quickly and came out to sit with them and watch the movie.

It was about a week after this incident that Tisha and Vihaan sat talking into the night in Vihaan's room. "There's something wrong with Maroof these days," Tisha said.

"What do you mean?" Vihaan asked though he could guess what Tisha might have to say.

"I might be wrong, I don't know. But I feel like he is avoiding us slightly. He refuses to travel with us to the office. He doesn't sit with us for too long during lunch."

"Yeah, I know," Vihaan realized.

"You do?" Tisha looked at him in surprise.

"Yeah, Amit has been teasing me a lot."

"Amit? About what?" Tisha was clueless.

"About us. You know, our relationship," Vihaan said casually.

Tisha jumped as if someone had just dropped a bomb on her. "How does he know?"

"They don't know anything." Vihaan rolled his eyes at her. "But the way we are. It isn't such a big task to guess what's going on here."

Tisha's face scrunched up in worry. She leaned into Vihaan. "I don't want to lose my friends."

"We are not losing them. They might just be giving us some space, that's all," Vihaan said reasonably. "Like good friends."

"Yeah, still," Tisha's voice was uncomfortable.

The next morning, Tisha was packing their lunch when Maroof was about to set off for office without Vihaan and Tisha. Tisha called after him, "Maroof, wait up. We are coming with you."

"You still need time to get ready, Tisha," Maroof said. "I'll be late."

"Nothing doing," Tisha demanded. "We are going together."

Maroof glanced at Vihaan, and Vihaan nodded at him with a smile. Maroof finally relented and sat down on the couch to wait for Tisha. Vihaan realized something very important about Tisha that day. Tisha liked to live in harmony, as a unit, and he would have to learn to become more accommodating for her sake. So, from that day on, he did his best to include Maroof and Amit more in their lives, and Tisha could only be happy about that.

Soon, Vihaan had made an itinerary for all the trips they could take in the next six months he had left in London. When he finally shared this plan with Tisha, she was silent for a while. Vihaan couldn't imagine what might be bothering her now, and he got a little miffed, afraid that all his plans would be wasted again. "What now, Tisha? Your family is not here to judge you."

Tisha shot him an angry glare. "I'm thinking about Maroof and Amit."

Vihaan was clueless. "What about them?"

"It has hardly been four months since I left Rehan. If they find out I've been in a relationship with you throughout this period, what will they think of me?"

Vihaan knew things could go out of hands if he said anything wrong, so he controlled his rising temper. "They will be happy for us. They are our friends. They will want what's best for us."

"Yes, you are right," Tisha said, and Vihaan knew from her tone this was not the last of it.

"What do you want to do then?" Vihaan asked, steeling himself to convince Tisha for his plans at any cost.

"We can ask them to come with us," Tisha said nervously, trying to read Vihaan's face. "Then it would look like a group of friends going out together. No one will point fingers at me then."

By then Vihaan was so desperate to go on a vacation with Tisha that he was willing to let even Maroof and Amit tag along with them. So, he agreed without further ado, knowing it would be easier to go along with her plans than to make her change her mind.

Maroof and Amit were very excited when they heard the plan. Soon, their bags were packed, and all the bookings were done. One fine day, they locked their house and set off for their first trip. The days and nights blurred into one another as they zigzagged from London to Budapest to Vienna to Prague to Berlin to Amsterdam. Each place had something different to offer and they made it a point to experience and explore as much as they possibly could within their schedule. Vihaan went around clicking hundreds of pictures everywhere they went. He and Tisha planned to make a collage with these pictures and put it up on a wall in their home after they got married. They drank the local beer at every place and made a note of what they liked best. Tisha also suggested Vihaan to collect the badge pins from every place to stick on his DSLR bag.

Vihaan's main motive behind arranging these trips had been to get closer to Tisha, and that was what happened. In all the newness and excitement around her, she loosened up a little bit more and stopped thinking about others, focusing solely on each other. They shared a room at every hostel they stayed in. Of course, Amit and Maroof had understood by then, but they didn't talk about it, and Tisha didn't seem to care either. Vihaan felt as if he was making more memories of Tisha to carry inside of him than of the places they were visiting.

They were in Amsterdam during the last leg of the trip, having lunch at a local restaurant, when they became acquainted with an Indian girl who was traveling alone. From Maroof's overt helpfulness, Vihaan realized that he was interested in her. So, he invited the girl to join them for the day. The five of them went around together all day, and they dropped her at her hotel at night before returning to their hostel.

Vihaan and Tisha were again sharing the two bunk beds in one room. Vihaan was almost on the verge of falling asleep when he felt someone sitting beside him. Alarmed, he hastily turned on the bedside lamp and saw Tisha beside him. She was looking morose for some reason.

"What happened?" Vihaan asked worriedly, sitting up and taking her hand in his.

"You were flirting with that girl today," Tisha said bluntly, her voice choked with tears.

Vihaan goggled at Tisha speechlessly for a moment. "No, I was trying to set her up with Maroof."

"Maroof?" Tisha's eyebrows puckered in confusion.

"Yeah, didn't you notice? He likes her. They have exchanged numbers also. You saw that."

"Oh!" Tisha sat silently.

Vihaan brushed his thumb over her wrist, in a soothing gesture. "There's no place for anyone else in my life, Tisha. It's just you."

Tisha looked into his eyes and nodded. Vihaan took her into his arms and they stayed like that for a while.

The next day was the last day of their trip. They met up with an ex-colleague, Roshan, who took them to smoke pot which was legal there. Then the five of them visited a red-light area for a few hours and then went back to smoke pot again. Vihaan and Amit got high quickly, but Tisha and Maroof didn't seem very affected by it. They were lounging in their seats, feeling at peace when Tisha said suddenly, "I want to say something."

Everyone looked at her. She went on recklessly, her nerves strengthened by the pot. "So, guys, the thing is, Vihaan and I have been in a relationship for the last couple of months."

Vihaan sat up straight, completely taken aback, and looked around at the others to see their reactions. But no one was falling off their chairs or looking perturbed in any way. They remained slumped the way they were a few minutes ago.

Amit said, "Yeah. We guessed."

Maroof added, "Good for you guys. You complement each other well in all ways."

Roshan asked, "Shall I order another round of pot to celebrate this news?" He looked around at everyone.

Everyone nodded enthusiastically and they spent the rest of the night together like that.

The next two months were spent on more vacations, and by the end of it, all Vihaan had collected over five thousand pictures in his DSLR. He and Tisha decided to visit Iceland, Croatia, and Rome again after getting married. And, they settled on Amsterdam as the location for their honeymoon since that was the place where Tisha had accepted Vihaan in front of everyone.

Part VII

August 2017

It was around August when London had started feeling like home. Vihaan and Tisha were returning in the evening after a badminton match with their colleagues. Amit had gone to India to attend a cousin's wedding, and Maroof had gone out to buy some chicken since in Amit's absence they were finally free to eat non-veg in the house. Vihaan and Tisha were in a good mood after a light-hearted match. But as they came closer to the house, what they saw brought them up short. The light was spilling out of Maroof and Tisha's windows that faced the main road. Vihaan knew Tisha could be careless and could have left the lights on in her room, but Maroof could never have done that.

Getting suspicious, he asked Tisha to wait outside on the front lawn and went up to Tisha's window to peek inside. The sight that greeted his eyes made his blood run cold in his veins. Her room was in a mess. The cupboard and the suitcases and the drawers were all lying opened. Her belongings were scattered haphazardly all over the room; on the bed, on the dresser, over the chairs, the study table, everywhere. Vihaan realized that there had been a burglary in their house, or maybe even something worse than that.

He immediately called the police. The police vans came within fifteen minutes. It was like a scene from a Hollywood movie where an entire police force comes to the rescue of the victim. By then Maroof had also come back.

The police officers made Vihaan, Tisha, and Maroof wait outside, while they went inside to search the house. They waited with bated breath to hear what had happened. After the search was completed, they were informed gravely that their house had indeed been robbed. They were escorted to their rooms and made to identify the stolen items. The sight of their upturned house was a shock to their system. Vihaan was heartbroken when he saw that his DSLR was gone along with a pair of Nike shoes he had bought for his brother-in-law. The only good thing was that Vihaan had already transferred the pictures on his DSLR to an external hard drive, so at least he didn't lose the memories along with the camera. The others had mostly lost their clothes along with some expensive perfumes. The police explained that it was a common perception in the area that Indians had a lot of gold in their house, and that must have been the reason why they were targeted in such a planned way. It was then that they found out that crimes, even murders, were commonplace in Hounslow.

That night Tisha was the most disturbed. Vihaan thought it must be because of the lost items, but later she explained, "You take work-from-home so frequently. What if you had been in the house when the robbers had come?"

Vihaan was moved by Tisha's concern for him in the face of her losses. He took Tisha in his arms and soothed her.

They had to move from Hounslow after that. All the door locks were broken in the house, and it would need a few days for the house to be repaired. Vihaan and Tisha moved in with Vihaan's manager, while Maroof shifted with some other friend of his.

Vihaan's manager lived in a 1 BHK flat with his wife. Vihaan and Tisha were treated like younger siblings by their host and hostess, and yet they couldn't get comfortable there. The loss of their home had given rise to a gnawing, ominous feeling inside them. They didn't discuss it openly, but they both could sense the unease in each other. Vihaan and Tisha had taken to sleeping on the floor while letting their hosts take the bed at night. They would stay awake late into the night, not talking, just sleeping beside each other and feeling comforted by each other's presence.

After the initial few days, Vihaan and Tisha started going out for late night walks. They would hold hands while walking and make plans for their future and promise to be there for each other at every point in life.

Somehow, these intimate moments with Tisha felt more real and more potent than everything else in his life. Every tension and every problem felt inconsequential when he held Tisha's hand and walked by her side.

Their house in Hounslow was soon repaired, and Maroof decided to return. Amit also joined him when he came back from India. But Tisha wasn't comfortable about going back again. So, Vihaan shifted with Tisha to the house in Wembley where he used to live initially after he had come to London. Now they had about seven other housemates, and Tisha felt safer among so many people. They didn't take very long to settle down there. Tisha had a way of befriending people very fast, and soon Vihaan and Tisha were sitting with their new housemates to watch movies on the television late into the night over beer and popcorn. And, with every passing day, Tisha was taking over Vihaan's responsibilities more and more–from his food to his clothes to his work to his moods and to his happiness–so that Vihaan could see nothing except Tisha anymore.

It was around October that Tisha came into Vihaan's room when he was working on his laptop. She lay down beside him. "I was just talking to Bali," she said.

"How's she?" Vihaan asked, engrossed in his work.

"Good," Tisha said. "She told mom and dad about us today."

Now Tisha had Vihaan's attention. He moved his laptop aside and turned to face Tisha. "Why did she have to talk to them? You should have done it."

"Don't be silly, Vihaan." Tisha sat up. "She is with them. She can handle them better right now."

"So, what did they say?" Vihaan's heart was suddenly thudding fearfully.

Tisha chewed her lips nervously. "They are angry."

Vihaan's eyebrows puckered. "Why?"

"Your caste," she mumbled.

Vihaan was rendered speechless. "I think you should talk to them personally," he said after a while, trying to pull up his courage. "Bali shouldn't have brought up the topic in your absence. She wouldn't be able to explain."

"She had to. Dad is looking for grooms. There's someone he liked. So, Bali had to talk to them."

Vihaan's heart sank even more. "Call your dad."

"Now!?" Tisha asked nervously.

"Yeah. See what he's saying."

Tisha hesitated initially, but on Vihaan's encouragement, she called her father's number and put the phone on speaker. But her father didn't answer the call. Getting worried, she called Bali instead. Bali received the call after a few rings. "Why isn't dad picking up his phone?" Tisha asked anxiously.

"He just had a fight with mom," Bali answered.

Tisha's eyebrows puckered. "About what?"

"About you, what else?" Bali sighed. "He thinks you broke his trust, and he was accusing mom for it."

"What does that mean? What has mom done?" Tisha had turned pale.

"He says mom couldn't raise you well. Dad thinks all the freedom he gave you has gone to your head," Bali explained.

There was silence on all ends for a while. There was a big hollow in the pit of Vihaan's stomach by now. He kept his eyes fixed on the phone desperately. "Did they say anything about Vihaan?" Tisha asked finally.

"No, when I tried telling him about Vihaan in the evening, he just got up and left the room. I didn't dare to talk to him after that. I think we should give him some time to cool down," Bali said wisely.

Vihaan couldn't stop himself from interrupting the conversation going on between the two sisters. "Don't do anything in a hurry, Bali. Talk to your mother first. See what she has to say about this."

Tisha added, "Yeah, mom can convince dad better than we can. Talk to her first."

Bali agreed with them. "Let me see. Mom is very upset right now. I'll talk to her soon."

"We are depending on you, Bali," Vihaan said with a desperate plea in his voice.

"I'll take care of everything, Vihaan," Bali promised.

After saying their goodbyes, Tisha disconnected the call.

Tisha was inconsolable that night. Vihaan could understand her problem. He had seen even the smallest of things making her frazzled. And, here her father was passing judgment on her. There was nothing Vihaan could say to lighten Tisha's heart. A leaden feeling of doom settled over Vihaan as well. But he tried to stay positive.

They held hands again and promised each other that they would fight till their last to convince their parents.

Days turned into weeks, and Bali kept informing them about the situation at home. Things seemed to be going from bad to worse. Tisha's father had taken to accusing and blaming her mother for everything. And, he was absolutely refusing to listen to Bali, so her mother was the only person Bali could talk to. Her mother would at least listen to Bali calmly, without flying off the handle, though Bali couldn't say what she might be actually thinking about the situation. Tisha, Vihaan, and Bali consoled each other daily that her mother could fix everything, that with time her father would come around.

Tisha was so scared of talking to her parents that she stopped calling them. They also didn't call her directly. Bali became the link between all of them. Vihaan could see Tisha's misery, and he tried his best to keep her cheerful. There was a time when she used to initiate their daily fun activities, now Vihaan took charge of that. He would drag Tisha out of the house whenever she wanted to stay holed up in her room. Whenever he would see her sitting silently, he would force her to watch movies or just chat with him. Tisha started sleeping in Vihaan's room every night now. The bleaker their situation became, the tighter they held onto each other, never letting each other go out of their sight for more than a few minutes.

Their friends came as a source of solace in all this. Vihaan and Tisha had grown a little distant from Amit and Maroof after they changed homes. But now Vihaan started arranging get-togethers every weekend. When Vihaan shared his woes with them, they also supported him. Everyone could see how perfect Vihaan was for Tisha. They emphatically told Vihaan and Tisha to stop worrying about this. They were sure that once they met Vihaan, they would change their minds. Vihaan and Tisha chose to believe them, and such reassurances from their friends lightened their hearts.

One night after returning from office, Vihaan and Tisha found out that their housemates were planning an impromptu picnic of sorts on their lawn. The sudden plan excited them and they started helping everyone with the arrangements. They were laughing and chatting with the others as they all went about their assigned duties. Vihaan and Tisha were helped by two other people in cooking dinner for seven people. Later, they all sat under the open sky and ate and drank to their heart's content, talking about cricket matches and politics and movies and celebrities–and the night flew away with the clinking of cutlery and the boisterous noise of carefree laughter.

Vihaan was about to go to bed much later that night when Tisha came running into his room. The tension on her face was like a harsh blow. Her phone was ringing in her hands with an ominous urgency and her hands were shaking. "Mom is calling," Tisha announced.

Vihaan's scalp prickled uncomfortably. "What are you waiting for? Talk to her."

Tisha nodded, chewing her lips again and pressed the receive option. "Hi, mom," she breathed into the phone, trying to be casual. She put the phone on the speaker so that Vihaan could hear the entire conversation.

"How are you?" Tisha's mother, Rupa, asked.

"Fine."

"Why don't you call me anymore? I always see Bali on the phone with you. Have you forgotten us already?" In spite of what the words would suggest, Rupa's voice was sad, not accusatory.

Tisha sat down on the bed, exhausted as if she was carrying the burden of the whole world on her shoulders. "I was afraid that you are disappointed in me like dad is."

Rupa was silent for a while. Finally, she asked, "Why didn't you tell us about Vihaan earlier?"

"I met him here in the London office, mom. I didn't know him before that. I didn't plan any of this," Tisha lied with full conviction.

Vihaan's eyebrows puckered in displeasure and he looked at her questioningly. Tisha shook her head, gesturing him to let her handle the situation. More worried now, Vihaan sat beside Tisha.

"Your father is very angry," Rupa said.

"But why, mom? Dad has never even met Vihaan or talked to him. Why is he judging him from so far away?" Tisha was losing her control slowly.

"Your father thinks you have betrayed him and kept him in the dark."

It was like a bomb had been dropped in the room. Tisha exclaimed in shock, "Betray! Choosing my own life partner is not betraying."

In the face of Tisha's indignation, Rupa remained calm. "After Rehan, we thought you will marry the guy we choose for you. Your father started looking for grooms, and he told all our relatives and friends to help. Now your father doesn't know what he will tell them. They will all laugh behind his back."

Tisha and Vihaan sat speechlessly, just staring at each other, all the breath knocked out of them.

"I want to talk to Vihaan once before I talk to your father," Rupa demanded.

Tisha looked at Vihaan. "Okay. I'll ask him to call you tomorrow morning."

"Okay," Rupa acquiesced.

"Mom," Tisha asked, holding her breath, "are you with me?"

"I want to talk to Vihaan," Rupa said simply, deflecting Tisha's question.

"Yeah, goodnight then. I...I need to sleep. Have to go to the office early," Tisha mumbled, hardly aware of what she was saying.

"Take care of yourself," Rupa said gently.

"You, too. Bye." Tisha disconnected the call.

"Why didn't you let me talk to your mother right now?" Vihaan asked as soon as the call had disconnected.

"Before you talk to her, we need to discuss what you will say," Tisha explained in irritation., "We have to be careful."

Vihaan nodded, agreeing with Tisha on this. "But do you think lying will solve anything? You said we met here. What if they find out the truth later from someone?"

"Who will tell them, Vihaan?"

"Could be anyone. Bali, our close friends, anyone."

"No one will be that foolish," Tisha brushed off his concern. "First Rehan was pointing fingers at me. Now, if I tell the truth at home, my parents will point fingers at me. They won't see you in a good light either. We can't tell the truth."

Vihaan didn't like this. He didn't want to build their relationship on the foundation of a lie, but these were her parents, so he chose to let her deal with them in her own way. But for now, everything seemed to be hanging on the phone call with Tisha's mother the next day.

Vihaan decided to work from home the next morning since he didn't know how long his conversation would last with Tisha's mother. He wanted space to talk freely to her. Tisha also wanted to stay, but she couldn't take a leave or work from home and she had to go. She wished him luck with a passionate kiss and stepped out of the house. Vihaan watched her walk down the street with growing dread.

Around noon, Vihaan called Tisha's mother. "Hi, aunty," he kept his voice as polite as he could, his heart drum-rolling inside his chest.

"Hello, Vihaan? How are you?" Rupa asked politely.

"I'm fine." Vihaan gulped nervously before continuing. "Tisha said you wanted to talk to me."

"Yes, I heard about you from Bali."

"Yes, Bali and I have talked a few times."

Rupa was silent for a few moments before speaking again. "Did Tisha tell you anything about our family? About her father?"

"Yes. I know he is angry."

"He is a difficult man, my husband. He takes his own decisions and never listens to anyone. That's just how he is." Rupa sighed. "He is not happy about this relationship, mostly because of your caste." Vihaan could detect the stress and the hopelessness in her voice, but she continued, "Anyway, Vihaan, it's also important to know what your parents have to say on this. Have you talked to your parents yet?" Rupa asked.

"My mother is a little sick right now. I'm going back to India in January. I'll talk to them then."

"Do you think they will agree?" Rupa asked sternly.

"I'll convince them," Vihaan promised, not too worried about his own parents.

"That means you are not sure yet?" Rupa's voice became cold.

"I'm absolutely sure my family wouldn't raise any issues on this. And, even if there is anything, I can handle it. Tisha is more important to me than anything."

"I see."

"Aunty, will you talk to uncle?" Vihaan asked. "Tisha is very disturbed by everything that is going on."

"I don't know what I can do. Her father is not a person who changes his mind easily."

"Yes, I got to know." The cold detachment in Rupa's voice was sapping Vihaan of all his strength. "Can I ask you something?"

"Yes."

"Why is uncle against Yadavs? Is there any bad history?"

"Nothing like that. He just wants the best for his daughters," Rupa answered vaguely.

"Aunty, I was born in Kolkata and I grew up in Nagpur. Then I worked in Mumbai and now I'm here in London. I've never even stayed in Bihar. I've just visited my relatives there a few times. That's all."

"I understand. But you must agree that no matter where we stay our blood never changes its color," Rupa said bluntly.

It was like a slap on Vihaan's face. He had never imagined someone could point fingers at his bloodline so heartlessly. Vihaan would never have taken this quietly had it been anyone else. But this was Tisha's mother, and their future was hanging on her decision, so he had to stay quiet and digest the insult.

"Look, Vihaan, my daughter is very emotional and impractical. She keeps taking decisions without thinking of the consequences." Rupa sighed. "I want my daughter to be happy. I will try to talk to her father."

This was what Vihaan wanted to hear, but he felt there were more things to come after this, so he held his breath. "I can't guarantee anything, Vihaan. If things don't work out, it will be better if you back out of this relationship."

Vihaan's heart sank, and yet he parroted, not ready to let go at any cost, not letting Rupa's words make home inside of him, "Uncle will listen to you, I'm sure of it."

"I'll try. That's all I can do. In the meantime, talk to your parents. If your family agrees then that might help us convince her father."

"I will, aunty. As soon as I go home." Vihaan disconnected the call after that and rang Tisha to let her know what had happened.

Vihaan had just two more months left In London after that. And, he was both dreading the end of his London tenure as well as getting impatient to sort everything out with his own parents. Bali continued relaying all the news from Tisha's home and nothing seemed to be changing. Rupa was failing to make any impression on her husband.

Vihaan and Tisha couldn't talk to her parents, so they kept rehearsing the arguments they would make in their defense whenever the situation arose. They reassured each other that no one could cut their logic: they loved each other and they were perfect for each other. It was what they told their hearts, and it was what their hearts told them. But unfortunately, it was the society's verdict that would determine their future, not their hearts. Deep inside they knew this truth, and this is what gave them sleepless nights.

All too soon, December was over, and Vihaan was ready to board the flight back to India. Tisha was trying not to get over-emotional, but Vihaan could feel her pain. Till now they were facing everything together, but now they would be alone for the next three months. Vihaan didn't want to depart on a sad note, so finally when he was about to set off for the airport, he handed Tisha all the parting gifts he had bought for her. Tisha was astounded to see the designer handbags, perfumes, watches, shoes, and whatnot that she had wanted to buy at one point of time. She couldn't believe Vihaan had remembered everything and bought them for her. Vihaan was simply happy to see the smile on her face.

Finally, when Vihaan had to walk away from Tisha for the boarding area, they held onto each other for a long time. The words of farewell wouldn't come to their lips, their eyes wouldn't stop looking at each other. Maroof and Amit had also come. They patted Vihaan and shook hands with him. With a final wave at everyone, Vihaan turned his back to London and walked away.

Part VIII

January 2018

Vihaan's heart was in his mouth on his birthday. He had chosen this day to talk to his family members about Tisha. It was his birthday, so he was hoping they would be more accommodating to his wishes. His mother, Renuka, and his sister-in-law, Priyanka, were busy cooking his favorite dishes for lunch. His two brothers, Ashwin and Arav, his sister, Prachi, and his brother-in-law, Saurav, were coming home to meet him. It was a festive atmosphere around him. Vihaan tried to participate in all the casual chatter going on in the house and look after his one-year-old nephew, Ayan, but it was still a great effort of will to control the restlessness and anxiety gnawing him from inside.

The moment finally came when the whole Kumar family sat down for lunch together. His brothers were tucking in the food without a care in the world. They all wanted to hear more about London. Vihaan kept regaling them with inconsequential events, slowly building up to the revelation. The plates were clearing up fast and Vihaan knew his moment had come.

"Something happened in London that I wanted to talk about," he said calmly.

Everyone looked at him normally, not expecting anything serious. His eyes fell on Priyanka and there was a small smile of understanding on her lips. Vihaan gulped and took heart from her smile.

Prachi teased him, "Got a foreigner girlfriend, did you, li'l bro?"

Vihaan blinked, momentarily amazed by the accuracy of his sister's guess. "Actually, yes. But she is not a foreigner. She is an Indian."

Prachi gaped. "I was just kidding."

Vihaan shrugged. "Turns out your joke hit the bull's eye." He looked around at everyone, and everyone was now peering at him with interest. His nervousness only escalated.

It was his mother, Renuka, who broke the silence. "Who's the girl?"

Vihaan looked only at his mother now. "Her name is Tisha Shukla. She was with me at the London office. She will be joining my Mumbai office when she returns in

April." He had set up this story with Tisha. "She is a very nice girl."

"She lives in Mumbai?" Renuka asked.

"Yeah. But she belongs to Jaipur. Her family is there."

Saurav asked, "Is she in your team?"

"No. She is in sales support, one level above me."

Saurav nodded. "That's nice."

"Show her picture, Vihaan," Prachi demanded. His brothers also nodded at Prachi's request. So, Vihaan pulled out Tisha's pictures on his mobile and handed the mobile to his sister. Everyone passed the phone around eagerly. Prachi passed the verdict. "She is definitely very beautiful."

"Who all are there in her family?" his mother asked.

"Her parents, one younger sister, and a younger brother. Her father is a senior manager in Steel India."

"They know about you?" Renuka asked the knottiest question of all, making Vihaan's heart sink to the pit of his stomach.

"Yes," he gulped before continuing, "but only her father is reluctant about our relationship. But I have talked to her mother and her sister, and they all are with us."

Kapil and Renuka shared a loaded glance. Their faces were hard and displeased. "What is her father saying?" Renuka asked.

"They are Brahmins," Vihaan announced. "He is against inter-caste marriage. We are Yadavs, so that's what his problem is."

Prachi got offended on her brother's behalf. "Why? How is my brother less than anybody else?"

Renuka's voice was grave. "It isn't about a single person. That is just how our society runs."

"Times have changed, mom," Ashwin spoke up on behalf of Vihaan.

"Yes, but not everyone is changing with the times," Renuka countered her eldest son. "Inter-caste marriage is still seen as a stigma. That is a reality."

Vihaan tried to explain calmly, "Mom, they are also open-minded people like us. Tisha's upbringing has just been like ours. She and her siblings have never faced any restrictions due to orthodox values. But yes, her father is being difficult this time, about this inter-caste marriage. We don't understand why. But with time he will get ready for this also, we are sure. Tisha's mother is going to talk to her father once you all give your consent to our relationship."

Renuka wasn't moved by Vihaan's argument. Her face became harder. Vihaan waited for her to say something, but without another word, she got up and left the room.

Everyone sat quietly in a state of shock. Vihaan appealed to his father now who had been silent throughout the conversation. "Dad!"

"Your mother is not wrong," Kapil said. "Her father is against inter-caste marriage. Even if we say yes, do you really think they will all be okay with this?"

"But dad, we love each other, and that's enough. We are happy with each other. True her father has some serious issues about caste, but Tisha and I, we will convince him.

We just need a little time." The stiffer Vihaan's opposition became, the more resilient he was getting.

Kapil stared at Vihaan for a moment, assessing his youngest son. "Give us some time to think about this." And Kapil also got up to leave.

Vihaan sat, feeling dazed. He had been afraid, true, but he had also believed deep down that his parents would agree. Now he didn't know what would happen next or what he would say or do next.

Saurav put his hand on Vihaan's shoulder, bringing him out of his stupor. "Let us talk to Tisha once."

Arav added, "Yeah, we should talk to her once before we all talk to mom and dad about you two."

Priyanka agreed. "We should get to know her first."

Vihaan smiled at his siblings. He could never tell them in words what their support meant to him.

That night Vihaan sat with his siblings to introduce them to Tisha over a video chat. He had told Tisha earlier what had happened and she was just as nervous as he was. But like always her nervousness didn't show as she greeted Vihaan's family with her usual cheeriness. Vihaan was a little relieved to see that Tisha was holding her own in front of his family.

But soon Saurav raised the topics that needed to be cleared before they could move ahead. "Tisha, are you aware of Vihaan's temper? He is very short-tempered and gets angry on small things."

Tisha smiled fondly at Vihaan. "I've seen him at it. We have been together for more than a year now. I know what he is like."

"You think you are okay with that?" Ashwin asked. "After all, you have to spend your life with Vihaan. You will either have to learn how to adjust or he will have to learn how to control himself. Neither of the two options is going to be easy. I wish Vihaan could learn to control himself."

"Hmm. I know how to deal with it. It doesn't take him too long to cool down when he loses his temper. And, then he himself comes and apologizes," Tisha reassured everyone.

Everyone laughed heartily at that.

"That's good then." Saurav smiled at Tisha happily. He thumped Vihaan's back jovially. "We are waiting to meet you when you come back to India, Tisha."

Tisha and Vihaan looked at each other for a moment, unable to find the words that would suit the moment of relief. But they could read the happiness in each other's eyes, and it was that unspoken connection that tied them together through every turmoil. Vihaan wished he could hold Tisha close at that moment and sighed heavily, knowing there were two more months to go before he could do that again.

Vihaan's siblings had just one thing to say after their chat with Tisha, that she was wiser than Vihaan. Vihaan beamed on hearing this. When he told this to Tisha later, she just looked smug and said, "So from now on you will have to listen to whatever I say. I'm wiser than you are, after all."

Vihaan pretended to doff his hat. "At your command, ma'am!"

Tisha giggled.

For the next one week, Vihaan's siblings kept talking to Vihaan's parents and after a lot of discussions, they finally agreed. But they had one request. They wanted to meet Tisha once she was back in India. Vihaan couldn't be any more thrilled.

Tisha informed Rupa that Vihaan's parents had given their consent. And, then Rupa started appealing to Tisha's father about Vihaan and Tisha's relationship. But he remained steadfast in his decision. So, by the time, Tisha arrived in India again in April 2018, nothing had changed in her family at all.

Vihaan went to pick Tisha up from the airport. Vihaan had already arranged for a new apartment where Tisha could move in. He had decorated the new place to welcome Tisha with fairy lights in resemblance to the old place she had in Mumbai. Tisha was touched when she came home with Vihaan and saw all the arrangements that he had done for her. Vihaan was also touched by what Tisha had brought for him from London. Tisha knew how disappointed he had been when his DSLR had been stolen, so she had gotten him a new one.

That night Vihaan took her out for shopping and a movie. From there, he took Tisha for a surprise candlelight dinner that he had arranged at a restaurant called The Bay View, where Tisha had always wanted to go. There were fancy food and fancy wine. Tisha kept getting more emotional than usual. They were together after a long time and she was moved to notice that distance only strengthened Vihaan's attachment to her. They held hands all through the evening, discussing about their happy moments and their happy dreams for the future. The anxiety about Tisha's father lurked inside them 24x7 now. But for one night they suppressed all that negativity and focused on each other, enjoying the feeling of holding each other again, of hearing each other's voices, seeing each other's smiles. It felt like the evening could stretch on forever but they would never have enough of each other.

Once Tisha joined office, another problem arose in the form of Rehan. This was the first time Rehan was seeing Tisha and Vihaan together as a couple, and neither Vihaan nor Tisha liked the nasty glares he threw at them whenever they crossed paths. Tisha had stopped talking to Rehan, and he also didn't try to cross his limits again. But the animosity he gave off whenever he was close by was disturbing for both of them, though they didn't discuss this openly. The challenges they were facing were much worse than Rehan's surliness. But through all this, their friends from the office came in the form of relief. Because finally they had told their friends about their relationship, and everyone was very happy for them. This unanimous support they got strengthened their belief that things would fall in place with time because they were meant to be together–just like everyone said.

Vihaan took Tisha to meet his parents in Hyderabad for one weekend in April. Everyone extended a warm welcome towards Tisha as if she was already a part of their family. They asked her about her family, about her interests, her childhood. Tisha shared her stories with Vihaan's family happily, and he could see the appreciation for Tisha grow in everyone's eyes. It was a joyous moment for Vihaan to see Tisha getting along so well with everyone. Kapil thought it prudent to discuss Vihaan's temper issues with Tisha all over again. Tisha reassured him confidently that she knew how to handle Vihaan's mood swings.

It was then that Renuka asked Tisha, "So, what did you like about my son, Tisha?"

Tisha glanced at Vihaan and gave him a small smile. "He is very caring about his friends and family. That's what I love the most about him."

Renuka smiled at Tisha and patted her hand gently. "There's nothing more we would like to see both of you happy."

"We need your blessings, aunty." Tisha smiled happily.

"But what about your father, Tisha? Do you really think you both can convince him?" Renuka asked somewhat gravely now.

"Yes, once he meets Vihaan, I'm sure he will come around," Tisha said confidently.

And finally, Tisha's confidence seemed to soothe all the anxieties in Vihaan's parents. They became more jovial and more talkative after that so much so that when it was time for Tisha to leave, Renuka insisted that they buy her some jewelry as shagun. Tisha got awkward at that, but Renuka and Kapil wouldn't budge.

So, Vihaan took his parents and Tisha to a jewelry store and Renuka asked Tisha to choose whatever she wanted to buy. They had a fun time after that browsing through the store, and finally, Tisha selected a pair of gold earrings for herself. Vihaan bought it for her and Renuka presented it to her with her hands in the form of blessings.

The spark had been doused at one end, but the wildfire was still raging on at Tisha's home. So, even with this victory, Tisha and Vihaan couldn't really celebrate absolutely after they returned to Mumbai. In fact, Tisha fell ill due to the constant anxiety eating her from inside. Vihaan stayed back at her place to take care of her. It didn't take them long to get swept up by the emotions, and before they knew they were in each other's arms, savoring each other and promising themselves to each other with silent kisses. The next morning, they woke up entangled in each other's arms, happy and peaceful. They just lay there with each other, looking into each other's eyes for an infinitely long moment.

As the days passed, they held hands now with more firmness and kissed with more passion, but their hearts wouldn't stop fluttering anxiously now and then as they looked at each other, wondering how the future would play out, since every other day they kept hearing how Tisha's father was hurling abuses at Bali and Rupa, how he was locking himself up in his room, how he was not eating properly, how he was refusing to interact properly with his family members. The news kept getting graver every day.

One day the news came that Tisha's father was hospitalized after his blood pressure fell suddenly. The doctor had said excessive stress was the reason behind his illness. Tisha became very nervous. She didn't want anything to happen to her father because of her. The night when they got the news Tisha and Vihaan sat together, deep in discussion. The discussion became graver the longer they talked. Tisha was feeling hopeless in the face of her father's failing health. Vihaan didn't know anymore what was right and what was not. He certainly didn't want to become the reason for anyone's ill health. In his moment of utter bleakness, Vihaan said, "Listen, we will stop fighting for our relationship if it endangers the health of our families in any way."

Tisha nodded, blinking back tears. "Yeah." She wrapped her arms around Vihaan while Vihaan wrapped her in his, letting their silence convey their desolation.

The next day, Tisha took a leave from work for a few days and went to meet her father in Jaipur. Something seemed to be stuck in Vihaan's throat all day as he waited for Tisha to call.

But Tisha's call never came. Unable to wait any longer, he called her around midnight. Her broken voice confirmed all the fears that were festering inside Vihaan.

"Dad says he will never accept you because of your caste. If you had belonged to any other caste, even Bhumiyaar, he would have been okay with it," Tisha said. "If you had been Brahmin like us. it would have been a breeze, Vihaan."

"What did you say to all this?" Vihaan's voice was dry.

"I couldn't say too much. He is really ill."

"So, now what?" Vihaan asked, forming the words with extreme difficulty.

"Don't know. The day after tomorrow there's a wedding in the family. Mom wants me to attend the wedding with them. I'm staying back. Let me see if I get another chance to talk to dad." Tisha sounded as dead as Vihaan felt.

Time seemed to have stuck as Vihaan waited for Tisha to come back. Her father was refusing to talk to Tisha after their fight last night. Tisha didn't really want to attend her cousin's wedding, but she was going only because her mother was insisting. Vihaan also felt it would be a good thing for her to keep her parents happy.

Tisha sent him her pictures after she got ready for the wedding ceremony. She was looking very pretty in the embroidered green velvet lehenga that she had bought with Vihaan in Mumbai. Vihaan wished he could see her as his bride sometime soon. But even this wish gave him another pang of anxiety and hopelessness.

It was around one at night when Tisha's video call came through on Vihaan's phone. Vihaan had gone to bed by then. Tisha's excited smile caught him off guard at first. He rubbed the sleep out of his eyes and sat up straighter, intrigued, "What's going on?"

"Dad said yes, Vihaan!" Tisha exclaimed.

Vihaan was confused. "Yes to what?"

Tisha's voice got a little miffed. "For our wedding, you idiot!"

Vihaan almost dropped the phone from his hand in shock. "What!" He blurted out, his heart jumping into his mouth, hardly able to believe his own ears.

"Yes! Yes! Yes! He said yes!" Tisha screamed with joy. Vihaan could see she was still at the wedding venue.

"How come? What happened?" A huge smile was breaking out on Vihaan's face now.

"I'm not sure, but I think he felt bad when he saw my cousin getting married today. She is younger than me, and still, she got married earlier than me. So, that must have influenced him somehow." Vihaan listened with rapt attention. "I was sitting with dad when the wedding was going on. He was looking really sad. I don't know what came over him, and he suddenly said that he was ready to accept you as his son-in-law."

Vihaan couldn't stop smiling. "This...this is amazing... Tisha, I..."

"But...Vihaan, there's a but," Tisha got serious all of a sudden.

Vihaan's heart thudded fearfully. "What now?"

"He says he will just be there for the wedding, but he won't participate in anything."

For Vihaan this was far more than acceptable, though he understood Tisha's pain. "This is more than we could have asked for, isn't it, Tisha? We convinced him for the wedding. We will get through the rest also," Vihaan said with all his heart.

Tisha nodded. "I love you, Vihaan." Her voice was cracking with emotions.

Vihaan smiled–from the bottom of his heart–after what felt like a long long time.

Part IX

Vihaan and Tisha were finally in the mode of celebration. They were watching the world through colorful glasses again. They became even more inseparable than before. They started looking for a new apartment in Mumbai where they could shift in together after their wedding. Their future had never looked so real. Their dreams had never been closer. They became particularly fond of browsing through home décor stores to pick up things for their future home. Vihaan could only encourage her with all his heart. They started planning more foreign trips after their wedding, not ready to settle down after just one measly honeymoon in the Maldives. There was a diamond ring that Tisha fell in love with one day when they were out shopping. It was costed at around three lakh rupees, so Tisha gave up on it. But like he had done in London, Vihaan made up his mind to save the money and get her the ring as a gift on their wedding as a surprise. They also started looking for a pre-wedding photographer. Vihaan was Tisha's favorite one, but then he was one of the subjects of the photographs so they had to get another person for the job.

Their excitement, their happiness was so palpable that their friends didn't need to be told that they had good news to share. Vihaan's siblings too were very happy for him. His parents were relieved to know that Vihaan was happy. His family had seen him go into depression after his first break up in college. They had been afraid of such an outcome again. So, they couldn't be any happier to hear the joy in his voice when he gave them the news.

Vihaan's father had only one request to all this. He wanted to meet Tisha's family formally and get to know them. Vihaan didn't think too much of it and conveyed the news to Tisha. It came as a shock to him when Tisha informed him soon after that her father was refusing to meet Vihaan or his family.

"Why?" Vihaan asked, aghast.

"He says he is not comfortable meeting your family. It's more than enough that he has given his consent, there's nothing more he can do for us," Tisha's voice was low as she said this.

Vihaan remained silent for a while, things getting jumbled up inside of him again. His father had made a very simple and fair request. He wanted to uphold his father's honor by fulfilling his wish. But he knew by then that there was no point in forcing Tisha's father for anything. His brain whirred frantically as he tried to come up with an idea.

"Your mom can talk to my family instead of your dad," Vihaan said finally. "At least that way there will be some communication between the two families, and my parents will feel more involved."

Tisha also agreed with him and immediately called her mother to discuss the matter. So, that was how the first connection was established between the Shuklas and the Kumars. Tisha's mother and her uncles did all the communication on Tisha's behalf. Though the Shuklas didn't agree to a formal meeting, Vihaan's father understood the situation and felt appeased for the moment.

But just because Tisha's father had given the consent, it didn't mean things had cooled down at her place. He continued misbehaving with his family. Tisha became very nervous one day when Bali conveyed of their father's latest outburst–"I don't want to drive a wedge between two lovers. But Tisha should forget us once she gets married."

Tisha didn't know If her father was serious or if he was venting his frustration as usual. Tisha called her mother to discuss this, but Rupa didn't have any words of comfort to offer. Rupa wasn't sure herself what her husband was thinking. All she knew for certain was that Tisha's father was still upset. Tisha didn't have the guts to ask her father directly about this, and she kept hoping that this would blow over.

Vihaan kept this quiet from his own family. But his father was starting to get ominous. One day Kapil told Vihaan directly that he didn't like whatever was happening. Kapil was sensing something fishy about Tisha's father's intentions. Vihaan didn't dare tell his father that he was spot on. All he could do was give his father false reassurances. But Kapil wasn't to be convinced so easily.

One fine day while talking to Rupa, Kapil requested that they hold a small engagement ceremony for Vihaan and Tisha. It would provide an occasion where the two families could meet, and moreover, the whole arrangement would become formal. Rupa declined the request. Supposedly, engagement ceremonies were not the norm in the Shukla family. All such rituals were conducted directly in the week preceding the wedding. Kapil couldn't budge Rupa on this point, and he remained disturbed by the thought that the two families would meet directly on the day of the wedding. It felt unnatural to him. Vihaan knew his father was right, but there was nothing he could do about it. Kapil understood his son's helplessness, and in spite of all misgivings, he let the matter rest.

Soon, Rupa requested Kapil to fix a date for the wedding. Kapil wanted to wait till next year and get Vihaan's elder brother married first. But Rupa refused to that. Tisha's father wanted to get Tisha married by the end of 2018, and he wouldn't wait for anything. Again, Kapil gave in to the demands of the Shuklas. He asked Rupa to go ahead and fix a date for the wedding according to their convenience.

As Vihaan and Tisha heard of all these incidents, the discomfort kept growing inside them. They could see how unfairly the scale was being tipped, but there was nothing they could do. They were just deeply thankful to Kapil for being so understanding and cooperative. Tisha would often tease Vihaan to become more like his father and stop being grouchy. Vihaan took this as a compliment and wished with all his heart that he could stay strong enough to support Tisha all his life, just the way she was being strong for him. He could see how much it was costing Tisha to go up against her father, and for that, he loved her, even more every day.

Around July, the wedding date was fixed as the 10th of December. After consulting with Vihaan's family, the Shuklas went ahead and booked the wedding venue in Bhopal. But they didn't give any proper reasons for it to Vihaan's family as to why they choose Bhopal. Tisha explained to Vihaan that her father felt if the wedding was done from Jaipur his image would be tarnished, so he wanted the wedding to be done somewhere far away from home. The Shuklas had lots of relatives in Bhopal, so her father had chosen Bhopal as a convenient location. This was another blow to Vihaan's self-respect. But by then, it had become more important for him to marry Tisha. He didn't let her father's prejudice get to him. He told his family only half of the explanation and hid the rest.

As the wedding date drew nearer, the preparations began in both the families. Under constant pressure from Rupa and the other relatives, Tisha's father finally consented to meet Vihaan. It was absolutely unexpected, and Vihaan was more nervous than excited. His father took charge of the situation immediately. This was the moment they had all been waiting for. Now that it was here, they wanted to utilize it properly. Vihaan and his parents traveled to Jaipur one fine day to meet the Shuklas.

And finally came the day when Tisha's family was supposed to come and meet Vihaan. Vihaan was nervous the whole morning. Like a teenage girl, he got fussy about his clothes. He kept rummaging through all the clothes he had brought for the occasion and still couldn't settle on anything. Finally, he wore each shirt he had with him and sent the pictures to Tisha. Tisha finally chose which shirt he should wear. Once this was done, he kept rehearsing in his head all the things he would tell Tisha's father about himself. No matter how much he prepared himself, everything just felt inadequate. He kept pacing in his room in agitation. He wished he could smoke to keep his nerves steady, but even that was not possible under the circumstances.

Tisha's father arrived with her maternal uncles at the hotel. Tisha's father, Dinesh Shukla, was just as scary looking in real life as Vihaan had imagined him to be. He had a perpetual frown on his face as if nothing he saw was good enough for him. When Vihaan greeted him by touching his feet, his eyes went even colder, though he did give Vihaan his blessings. Vihaan's heart only sank further. But Tisha's uncles were friendly and polite, and it was their presence that bolstered Vihaan's confidence. They all greeted each other cordially, though Dinesh didn't drop his stiffness.

Vihaan took them to his room and ordered tea and breakfast for them. And, then their conversation began. It was Tisha's uncles, Ramesh and Sailesh, who did all the talking. Dinesh remained silent, assessing every word that Vihaan said, every move he made. Vihaan tried to appear confident, but he couldn't understand from any of their faces what impression he was making.

Ramesh said to Vihaan, without beating about the bush, "Have you thought carefully before deciding to marry Tisha?"

"Yes, uncle." Vihaan nodded confidently.

"If anything goes wrong then you both will be responsible for it," Ramesh warned, keeping his tone gentle.

Vihaan knew this already. "Of course, uncle, Tisha and I love each other. This is our decision, and all the consequences too will be our responsibility."

Now Kapil addressed Dinesh directly, "Please ask Vihaan whatever you want to know."

It was Sailesh who spoke this time, "It's fine. Our kids have taken their decisions. What's left for us to know after that?"

Kapil nodded. Vihaan didn't know if this was a good thing or bad, even though this was a fair summation of the situation.

Ramesh said, "Many of our relatives have come down to meet you all. It would be great if you visit our home in the evening. You will get to meet the rest of our family there."

Vihaan's heart leapt in joy at the invitation. Kapil also smiled graciously. "That will be great."

"That's settled then."

It was decided that Vihaan and his parents would visit Tisha's home in the evening that day. Tisha's father left soon with her uncle, and Vihaan heaved a sigh of relief. He had been dreading this moment for months, and finally it was over and everything had gone well. But for some reason, he noticed a frown on his father's face. In the face of his relief, he chose to overlook it.

That evening, Vihaan and his parents arrived at Tisha's house with the customary gifts. They were welcomed and greeted cordially by her family. Vihaan again got nervous to see so many relatives from Tisha's side. But his anxiety was dissipated the moment Tisha came out to meet Vihaan. She was dressed in a pink suit with large danglers. She was looking beautiful beyond words. The soft smile on her face and the twinkling shyness in her eyes was an oasis of calm amid all the madness around him. As the elders talked among themselves, Tisha and Bali often winked at Vihaan whenever nobody was looking their way. Vihaan controlled his smile lest someone noticed what was going on.

Dinesh stayed quiet in the beginning, a fact that Vihaan and his parents noticed but again chose to overlook. As the conversation continued, Dinesh would leave the room with his brothers sometimes and return a little later. Vihaan couldn't understand what was happening. But since his father did all the talking on his behalf he just sat quietly. No one had anything to ask him, and he sat there observing everyone's reactions, feeling uncomfortable and overlooked.

In the middle of the conversation, talk moved to the wedding venue. Kapil asked, "You hail from Jaipur then why are you getting the wedding done from Bhopal?"

Now Dinesh spoke up finally. This was his decision after all. "Most of our relatives stay there. It would be a convenient thing." He continued, "The venue doesn't matter. You want our daughter; you can get the wedding done even from Hyderabad if you want. It hardly makes any difference to us."

There was pin-drop silence in the room after this. Dinesh's stance on this wedding became crystal clear to everyone at once. Vihaan realized that his father had inadvertently touched a nerve.

Kapil gathered himself and replied, “That is true. We want our kids to be happy. It doesn’t matter where the wedding happens.”

This seemed to open Dinesh up, for he entered the conversation now. Dinesh asked Kapil, “The surname, Kumar, is also used by the Bhumiyars in Bihar. But you are Yadavs. Is that right?”

Vihaan didn’t really like this question, but this curiosity was fair, he told himself. Kapil didn’t let himself get frazzled, and he explained how his own grandfather had adopted this surname in Kolkata and how it had stuck since then. Dinesh didn’t have anything to say to that.

Dinesh’s next question was, “So, Bihar is your native place? Do you still go there a lot?”

Kapil replied, “No, no. Maybe twice or thrice a year. When there’s some family function or maybe for the maintenance of the house.”

An interest seemed to flicker in Dinesh. “Oh, so you have a house in Bihar!”

Kapil nodded. “Yeah, we do. It’s a family inheritance.”

Dinesh was now on a roll. “And, in Hyderabad?”

Kapil explained, not sensing anything amiss, “Yes, we have our own house in Hyderabad also. Our eldest son bought it.”

Dinesh frowned, looking displeased again. “I see.” Dinesh’s voice had gone colder than before.

Again, the condescending tone was clear, though Vihaan didn’t realize what was so disappointing about what his father had said. An ominous feeling started to grow inside Vihaan now.

Kapil said to Dinesh now, earnestly, "Our children have chosen each other. Nowadays, youngsters fall in love and get married without even bothering to tell their families. But we have raised our children with proper values. They respect us and care about our feelings, so they came to us to ask for permission instead of just eloping. Now we have to give them their happiness. At first, we were also apprehensive about this relationship. But then we met Tisha and we really liked her. We are immeasurably glad that you have given your consent. My only request to you is that you should let go of all your resentment and give these children your blessings."

Dinesh nodded again but said nothing.

The silence became awkward. Tisha suddenly broke down, much to everyone's surprise and she ran out of the room. Vihaan got worried and he gestured Bali with his eyes to go after Tisha. Bali followed her sister out of the room. She soon came back and reported that Tisha was overwhelmed by everything that was going on. Vihaan understood her emotions very well. He wished he could go and soothe Tisha at that moment.

It had been almost two hours since Vihaan had arrived there. Ramesh requested Vihaan and his parents to join them for dinner at a nearby restaurant. But Kapil denied politely and they left for their hotel.

Sure, things hadn't gone smoothly, but Vihaan was sure they had done the best they could. His father had been polite and gracious, and he had made his interest in Tisha very clear. He didn't think Tisha's father would find anything more to complain about. In fact, that night he was more worried about Tisha than about her father. He had left her crying. He wanted to know how she was doing. He called her around eleven, assuming that everyone else in her place must have gone to bed by then. But Tisha disconnected his call and texted instead: Call you tomorrow.

Vihaan couldn't imagine for the world of him what this could be about. Convincing himself that she was tired or she was with some relatives, he let the matter rest and went to sleep.

The next day, Vihaan took his parents for sightseeing around Jaipur. They were in the Birla Temple when Tisha called. Vihaan went aside to attend her call.

"Is everything all right?" he asked Tisha worriedly.

"No. Everything has been going wrong again."

Vihaan's heart sank. He had been dreading this since last night. "What happened? I thought things went well at your place."

"There's something I didn't tell you," Tisha said.

"What?"

"After you left yesterday my father argued a lot with everyone who supports you." A leaden feeling of doom settled inside Vihaan the longer he listened to Tisha. "He says there is a huge difference between the standards of our families."

"What does he mean by standard?" Vihaan asked, unable to process this constant up and down.

"I don't know," Tisha said in a dead voice. "He didn't explain. But after he came back from your hotel, he said that he didn't like your appearance either."

"What was he expecting? Ranbir Kapoor?" Vihaan joked wryly, his heart-breaking withinsult and pain. "You told your father everything about me, right? He agreed after knowing everything. So, now what is his problem?"

"Don't know. My cousin who got married that day; she also did an inter-caste marriage with a Baniya guy. But that guy is filthy rich. Maybe dad thought you will be something like that." Tisha explained morosely.

"But that's not the truth, is it?"

"No. Dad doesn't like the fact that you are one level below me and even after your promotion you will earn the same as me."

"So, what now?" Vihaan asked.

"My uncles tried a lot to reason with dad, but he wouldn't listen to them. My uncles went back home last night after their fight." Tisha's voice was choked. "I don't know what to do now."

Vihaan forced himself to speak out loud. Everything inside him had become hollow. It was a miracle he was still standing on his feet. They had come so far only to be thrust back to the point where they had begun. "Let's give him time to calm down. Then we have to talk to him again."

"Hmm." Tisha could hardly speak.

Part X

For Vihaan and Tisha, Bali and Rupa had been the rocks in the turbulent sea. With Dinesh changing his stance all over again, they had no choice but to fall back on these two women in Tisha's family. But even they were failing to make any headway with Dinesh who continued with his rough behavior and his tantrums. Vihaan and Tisha were becoming more and more helpless with each passing day.

In the meantime, Tisha gave Vihaan a piece of news. Bali had found someone on a matrimonial website and she was dating him. Vihaan was very happy to hear the news. Bali had been upset with her back problems for a long time now. She was unable to do a job because of that, and it was a major setback for her. It was a good thing that she had found somebody. Vihaan made it a point to congratulate her personally. Bali sounded very excited about her relationship. Tisha had only one wish for her sister that she should never go through the kind of ups and downs she was facing.

And, it seemed Tisha's wish had come true. Tisha told Vihaan how excited her parents were about Bali's relationship with Kshitij. Kshitij was a manager withHonda. He had his own car. He lived in his own apartment in Delhi. He was also a Brahmin and he had no issues with Bali's health issues. He didn't care that Bali was not a working woman. He was giving her the freedom to become a housewife if that's what she wanted. He was Bali's dream guy. In short, he was everything that the Shukla's wanted their sons-in-law to be, and he was everything that Vihaan was not.

Vihaan and Tisha were genuinely happy for Bali. Bali would sometimes call them and tell them about Kshitij. They could see that Bali's focus was now completely on her boyfriend, and the more involved she got with Kshitij the more she started neglecting Tisha's problems. But Tisha and Vihaan couldn't bring themselves to dump all their worries on Bali, especially not when she was so happy.

Vihaan was about to go to bed one night when Tisha called him. Her voice sounded frantic. She wanted to meet him immediately, and she refused to say anything on the phone. With his heart in his mouth, Vihaan took a cab and reached Tisha's place. Tisha was looking worse than she had sounded on the phone. Vihaan sat her down and asked, 'What's wrong?"

Tisha stared into his eyes defeatedly for a moment. "I don't think Bali will support us anymore."

Vihaan's heart sank to the pit of his stomach. "Why?"

"She told Kshitij everything about us. And Kshitij has now placed a condition," Tisha explained.

Vihaan's eyes bored into hers. Tisha held his hands, needing support to keep talking. "He said his parents won't let him get married in a family that is associated with an inter-caste marriage."

"What! Why?" Nothing was making sense to Vihaan anymore.

"Orthodox values, maybe." Tisha gave a hollow laugh. "These people will fit in right with my father, huh?"

"What's Bali's stand in this?" Vihaan asked, still trying to find a loophole through which they could climb out. "She promised us that she would help."

Tisha sighed deeply. "That was when she wasn't in love. Now she has her own future to think of."

"So, she is asking you to leave me?" The shock was refusing to recede.

"She didn't say it directly. But she's my sister. I know her. She was very upset when we talked on the phone. She said there's no way she is going to leave Kshitij. She will never find a better guy than her."

"That's nonsense! How could he place such atrocious conditions? Does Bali really think he will be good for her in the long run?" Vihaan burst out.

"Yeah," Tisha nodded, "you are right."

"Talk to her. Make her see sense, Tisha. Ask her to explain the situation to Kshitij properly. What right does he have to interfere in your life? How do your choices matter to his family?"

Tisha agreed to talk to Bali the next day. But it was as Tisha had guessed. Bali was now stuck on Kshitij. Nothing that Tisha or Vihaan said made an impression on her. She believed Kshitij was the right man for her, and she refused to listen to anything against him. Vihaan and Tisha had hit a dead-end. When their friends heard about this, they were also stunned. This didn't seem to make sense to anyone. And, yet there was no way past this.

Bali and Tisha started having regular fights now. A wedge had been driven between the two sisters. Tisha's parents refused to interfere in the matter. It seemed to Vihaan that Tisha's father was now intentionally letting the clash between the sisters run its own course.

Tisha was now constantly on edge. There was no way she could tell Bali directly to dump Kshitij because then Bali could ask her to dump Vihaan. So, she tried to reason with Bali as rationally as she could, but Bali was in too deep with her man. Since Tisha couldn't vent out on Bali, all her frustration came out when she was with Vihaan. Vihaan was always the one with the temper issues, but now Tisha also started becoming short-tempered. They would fight over the most inconsequential things like where to go out for dinner. Vihaan knew Tisha's anger was not directed towards him, but even he was too wound up to handle the constant skirmishes with Tisha calmly.

A day came when Bali told Tisha directly that there was no way their father would accept Vihaan, so it would be better if Tisha left him and moved on. And, soon

Tisha's mother said she wanted to cancel the wedding venue for Tisha and Vihaan's wedding. When Tisha told Vihaan about this, he had no choice but to agree, but now Vihaan knew it was time to appeal to Rupa because clearly Bali had gone over to the dark side and things were spiralling out of control. After consulting the matter with Tisha, Vihaan himself called Rupa. Gradually the discussion between Vihaan and Rupa moved on to how unfair Kshitij's demands were.

"Aunty, do you really think Kshitij is the right guy? He is making such unfair demands to Bali even before they are married. He can't even make his parents see the reason now. Who knows if he would support Bali in the future if it comes between Bali and his family," Vihaan said.

But Rupa was strangely on Bali's side. "It is not Kshitij's fault, Vihaan. It isn't his demand. His family will raise objections if Tisha does an inter-caste marriage."

"But aunty, today they are trying to dictate Tisha's marriage. Tomorrow they will try to dictate the lives of her children! That doesn't make sense," Vihaan was losing his temper, but he tried with all his might to keep his voice polite.

"See Vihaan, you know all about Bali's health issues. She doesn't do a job either. And, nowadays everyone wants a working girl. We have been looking for a groom for Bali for a while now. No one showed any interest when they heard about her problems. But Kshitij is different. He has no issues with Bali's condition. This is the only demand he has placed. How can we reject him based on just one thing? And, moreover, Bali likes him. She will be miserable without him."

"Then what about us?" Vihaan asked. Everything had become hollow inside him. Bali's three-month-old relationship had suddenly become more vital than Tisha's two-year-old relationship. "What about Tisha's happiness?"

"Tisha is a bright girl." There was no hesitation in Rupa's voice as she spoke as if her mind was already made. "There won't be any problems in finding grooms for her."

"What does that mean, aunty?" Vihaan forced himself to say, understanding Rupa's meaning, but unable to accept it.

"Vihaan, you are also a very bright boy. You will find very nice girls. But I think you should move on now."

Time seemed to come to a standstill as Vihaan digested these words. He had promised Tisha that he would fight till the very last and he hung on desperately. He couldn't imagine the alternative of fighting. What would happen if he let go? Just the mere thought brought him up short and clogged his brain. "Aunty, we can look for more boys. This is an arranged marriage. We just can't get fixated on one person. We have to keep our options open."

Rupa sighed. "We have looked. There is no point. We will not get a better choice for Bali."

"Let me try, aunty, please," Vihaan pleaded, not even sure of what he would do next.

"Okay, try then," Rupa acquiesced reluctantly.

When Tisha heard about what her mother had said, she fell silent. Vihaan also had nothing to say. But he didn't want to waste any time. He opened online profiles for Bali on various matrimonial websites and started browsing for suitable grooms. When Tisha asked him what he was doing, Vihaan explained what he had promised her mother. Tisha sighed hopelessly. "Bali really does have a lot of problems. And, a lot of demands. You really think you can find someone better for her?"

Vihaan flared up and rounded on her. "So, what do you want me to do? Sit on a chair with my legs up? Forget that I love you? Cry all my life?"

Like so often these days, Tisha's anger was also at the boiling point. "Why are you shouting at me? I am just telling you how things are."

"Why can't you talk to your family and make them understand? Bali has made her stand clear. Why can't you do the same?" Vihaan hollered at her, reigniting the same old argument that had been going round and round for weeks now with no resolution in sight.

"I try, Vihaan. You know I try," Tisha sounded desperate. "I don't know what else I can say to make them listen to me."

Vihaan tried to brush off the argument. He pulled the laptop towards him again. "I don't know how long I can take all this drama."

"All you care about is yourself, Vihaan. Have you tried to understand what I am going through?" Tisha wasn't ready to let go of the argument. "Do you care about my problems?"

"I don't care about you?" Vihaan's eyebrows puckered angrily. "Then what am I fighting for?"

"You have a weird way of showing it."

"How so?" Vihaan demanded to know. "Here I'm running around to keep all your family members happy. That isn't enough for you?"

"Are you holding me responsible for all this? I am just as worried as you are. And, you are still shouting at me! What can I do if my family members are so difficult? Can't you be a little patient?"

"I haven't been patient?" Vihaan burst out. "I have been listening to all sorts of nonsense for almost a year now. I have digested every insult that your family threw at me. Now I am trying to help your stupid sister. What else can I do, Tisha?"

"Don't you dare insult my sister like that!" Tisha raged.

Vihaan immediately realized he had crossed his limit. They sat glaring at each other. It was a real effort for Vihaan to calm himself down. In a resemblance of politeness, Vihaan took Tisha's hand. She tried to pull her hand away. Vihaan held on to her tighter and pulled her close. "Let's forget this, okay?"

Tisha stared into Vihaan's eyes for a long time and finally nodded. But she was still disturbed. "Vihaan, you should leave for tonight. I want to go to bed early."

This was the first time Tisha had asked him to leave like this. It made him angry. Throughout the next month, they were both constantly at loggerheads, so much so that their friends also got alarmed by their state. Vihaan wanted to find a middle ground. He kept telling Tisha that she should ask Bali to get a job so that one of her setbacks got removed at least, and they could widen their search for the groom. But Tisha refused him flatly. Bali wanted to be a housewife, and Tisha didn't want to interfere in Bali's choice. Slowly Tisha was getting tired of fighting with her family and Vihaan was getting disturbed by her despondency. She was giving up. Vihaan could see that and he just wanted to push her to fight on.

As the days passed, the distance between Vihaan and Tisha started increasing. Tisha started refusing to spend too much time with Vihaan. She started avoiding his phone calls. When Vihaan broached the topic, she said she needed a break from all the bickering. Intense fear erupted inside Vihaan. He threw himself crazily into a groom search for Bali. He started making a list of suitable men from the various matrimonial websites. He then passed on the list to Tisha. It was agreed between them that Tisha would talk to each of these men and select the best candidates among them and talk about them with her family. But Tisha rejected most of the men he chose for Bali. She knew her father would not accept anyone who earned less than an annual package of fifteen to twenty lakhs. But Vihaan kept insisting that there was no harm in looking at men who earned in the range of ten to fifteen lakhs because in IT companies that package would definitely double within two years.

The fights between Vihaan and Tisha would ensue again whenever these issues came up. Vihaan couldn't understand for the life of him how anything could be achieved if everyone remained stuck to their stubborn demands. This was a sensitive issue and everyone had to make compromises, but no one was ready to move an inch from their places.

It was on the night when Tisha hung up on him in the middle of an argument that it hit home hard that Tisha was drifting apart from him, and this only fuelled his desperation to hold on.

Vihaan knew he had to stop their fighting. It was doing them no good. He kept asking her out on dates just so that they could talk like they used to before. But Tisha refused, again and again, giving different reasons each time. Vihaan decided not to push her at the moment and give her some space to cool down. He told himself that things would become normal with time though he had no solutions in sight.

But after a few days of this, Vihaan realized that Tisha had not been talking to any of the men he had selected for Bali. When he confronted her about this, Tisha got surly. "There is no point. My family has settled everything with Kshitij."

Vihaan was aghast. "What! Your mom said she would talk to other guys if I found anyone suitable. How can she go back on her word? What about us now?"

Tisha refused to look at Vihaan, suddenly getting interested in her nails. "Dad gave me two options. I have to choose between you and my family."

Vihaan could feel his whole world crashing around him. "Come on! He has been making such threats for a year now. He will come around, Tisha. He has to."

"No. He won't. And, I can't be selfish and ruin my sister's happiness."

"And, our happiness?" Vihaan wanted to shake Tisha. He wanted to rage at her. But he could hardly even make himself talk to her straight.

"You should move on, Vihaan. It's the best option for both of us." With that, Tisha walked out on Vihaan.

Vihaan sat quietly, dazed, his ears buzzing. He didn't know when he got up or when he left the office or how he reached home. He couldn't feel himself anymore. All he felt was the consuming pain that was burning him alive.

The next day in office, Vihaan went up to her in the Break Out Area but she walked away without even a smile. And, from then on, Tisha started avoiding Vihaan. She stopped replying to his calls and his messages and his emails completely. He couldn't even force her to talk to him in the office and create a scene. There were so many times when he just wanted to barge in at her place and demand an explanation and make her see sense. He wanted to accuse her for playing with his emotions. He wanted to remind her of the promises they had made to each other. But he couldn't really make himself behave like a deranged stalker. A restless fire kept burning him every second of that day now. Even his sleep was haunted by nightmares. In spite of all this, Vihaan kept up hope. He would wake up every morning and tell himself that today Tisha would talk to him. But each day passed by and nothing turned into more nothing.

The silence from Tisha had seeped so bone-deep into Vihaan that he started avoiding his friends and his family members as well. He hardly talked anymore, except for discussing work at the office. There was a time when Tisha and Vihaan used to greet each other politely if they ever bumped into one another at the office. But now life had come full circle. They still kept bumping into each other. The only difference was that now they didn't have any more greetings to one another.

One night during this period Vihaan was returning home from work in an auto. He had been seeing Tisha laugh and chat with her teammates as if nothing had happened, as if she was perfectly happy. He couldn't stop wondering if he had really meant anything to Tisha or if everything had been a show. His head told him something, but his heart rebelled to all logic, clutching on to the belief that their love had been real. The burning sensation inside him had become a constant thing now. But he had stopped thinking too much about these anxieties. From his previous experiences, he knew what to expect from a breakup. So, whenever the anxiety, the pain became too much, he would tell himself that with time this would pass away gradually.

But on this night, all of a sudden, he started feeling hot inside the auto, although the wind was cool. He started sweating and a sharp pain exploded in the middle of his chest. Fear lapped inside him. He wondered if he was having a heart attack. He couldn't understand what was happening to him. He gulped in air to calm himself, he drank water from his bottle, but the pain refused to subside. It was slowly becoming difficult for him to hold himself straight anymore. Gripped by panic, he asked the auto driver to take him to a nearby hospital.

Once Vihaan was in the hospital, the doctors first made sure that he was not having a heart attack and then he was sent to consult a psychiatrist who, on hearing everything, prescribed him 0.5mg of Clonazepam to calm his nerves and his brain. Vihaan was shocked to learn he was having panic attacks. He was advised to avoid stress, to relax, to go out on a holiday if need be and take a break from work because this was a serious issue. It would impact his health further if he neglected it. Vihaan came home in a state of denial. He had dealt with a break up before, and he could do so again, he believed.

Vihaan bought the prescribed medications, but he didn't take the pills. He kept seeing Tisha in the office every day and as the doctor had warned, his condition kept deteriorating. One day his fingers would swell for no apparent reason, one day his whole body would start paining, Vihaan couldn't keep track of what was happening to him anymore.

Vihaan kept all of this to himself, refusing to listen to the warning signs from his body, and threw all his focus into his work. He wanted to find an escape, and work was the only distraction he had, and on the third of January, his much-awaited promotion was announced. He dithered all day, trying to decide if he should really share this news with Tisha. His joy didn't feel complete as long as he didn't share it with Tisha. By the end, he couldn't stop himself. That night he went up to her when she was leaving the office.

"Hey, Tisha," Vihaan said, trying to appear bright, not letting the awkwardness get the better of him. "How are you doing?'

"Fine," Tisha was a little taken aback to be stopped by Vihaan so suddenly. She was looking uncomfortable. "How are you?"

"Good." Vihaan gave a vapid smile. "Great in fact! I got a promotion."

"Oh! Great." Tisha shook hands with Vihaan. It was a long time since Vihaan had been this close to Tisha, and he savored the moment.

"Shall I drop you home tonight? We can have dinner somewhere on the way back," Vihaan plucked up his courage and made the offer.

Tisha immediately backtracked. "No, Vihaan, it wouldn't be appropriate." Tisha didn't wait for another moment and strode out quickly.

Vihaan somehow dragged himself outside. He was waiting for a cab or an auto when he saw Tisha getting into an auto nearby. He ran towards her without thinking of right or wrong. Tisha was again awkward on seeing him there.

"You mind giving me a lift?" Vihaan requested.

Tisha didn't know how she could get out of this without being rude. So, reluctantly, she agreed. "Fine, hop in."

As the auto moved through the busy road, Vihaan's brain whirred frantically. He was finally alone with Tisha. He wanted to say something. He wanted to salvage their relationship. But he was coming up blank. Tisha was determined not to pay him any attention as if he wasn't even there. She wasn't even looking his way. The auto driver suddenly turned on the music player and the song Dekha Hazaron Dafa Apko came on. It unfurled a world of memories inside Vihaan and his eyes watered. He hastily blinked back the tears. He looked at Tisha, certain that Tisha would be affected by the memories too. But right then her phone rang. Tisha received the call. He couldn't hear who was on the other end. He just heard Tisha's clipped responses as if she didn't want to talk openly in front of Vihaan. Someone was demanding to know about Tisha's day and she was giving the person a detailed account of what she had done in the office, where she was, what she would do after going home, and so on.

When Tisha disconnected the call finally, Vihaan asked her, "Who was that? Your mom?"

"No." She still didn't meet his eyes.

"Bali?"

"No." Tisha breathed in deeply, steeling herself. "I'm seeing someone. My father has chosen a few guys for my marriage. He is one of them."

A pain seared in Vihaan's chest, and he didn't respond.

When Vihaan stumbled back home, he couldn't remember if Tisha had said anything more to him. He fell on his bed, fully clothed, feeling numb. The pain inside his chest was unbearable now. And, as he lay, listening to the sounds from outside, slowly he started feeling a strange tingling in his extremities. He tried sitting up, but his body wouldn't move. Panic, like he had never known before, pulled him in and he felt himself drowning in an undefinable, unknown darkness. It wasn't just his life that he had lost control of; now his body was betraying him too.

Two hours later when he was able to get up again, he packed his bags and left for Hyderabad that very night to meet his parents. The loneliness in his house was coming to bite him. And, he also had to find out what was happening to him. There was just one thing he knew now. He couldn't see Tisha again or be anywhere near her again. He didn't have the strength to see her and know she was lost to him, that she would belong to someone else now. He wanted to get rid of her memories, of the burn inside him, and staying in Mumbai would have meant living with her memories day in and day out. So, he ran away, away from his life, from his job, from Tisha, from himself.

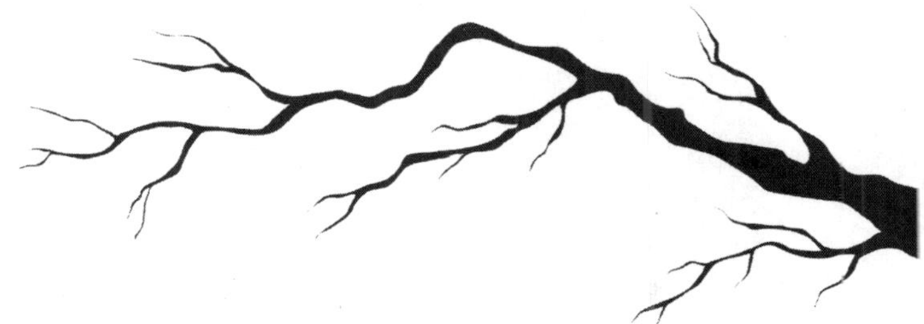

Part XI

January 2019

Kapil and Renuka sat beside Vihaan, none of them looking at each other, none of them having anything to say, each of them realizing their world had crashed around them. Vihaan had just recounted the whole story to his parents. He had just told them about his health condition. They had never heard of a panic attack disorder or depression before, and it took Vihaan some time to explain what exactly was happening to him. The horror was too much for Kapil and Renuka to absorb.

Kapil asked, coming out of his stupor, "What is the doctor saying?"

"Don't take any stress," Vihaan mouthed inaudibly.

Vihaan peered at his parents balefully, realizing that words would never convey his situation to others. A world of distance had creeped up between him and his parents now. Yes, his parents knew he was in pain, but they didn't really understand. Everything was happening to him; he wasn't making anything happen. All Vihaan could say was, "I don't know what to do." Vihaan was feeling numb from inside. "Everything is falling apart inside of me. I feel like I have lost everything. The hollowness has crawled inside him. Everything has ended."

"Nothing has ended. You will get better with time, and you will get all the happiness in the world." Renuka's voice was steel. Vihaan had left all hope, but Renuka wouldn't let him give up on himself. "We all love you. We are here for you. You are not alone, dear."

"I know," Vihaan said and hugged his mother. "I don't want to go back again."

"You don't have to," Renuka said. "Stay with us. All of us will stay together like we used to before." After some silence, Renuka said, "Don't think about those things anymore. Just relax at home for a few days."

"Are you taking any medicines?" Kapil asked the more important question.

"Not yet," Vihaan admitted his mistake. It was only now that he was realizing what a big mistake he had made in neglecting his health from the beginning.

"Then I'll get your medicines right now. You should start taking them immediately." Kapil got up purposefully. "Give me your prescription."

By the time Kapil came back from the medicine shop, Vihaan was in the throes of another panic attack. Renuka sat by his side, looking horror-struck and helpless as Vihaan lay beside her paralyzed, unable to even utter a single word. He saw his mother crying beside him, but he couldn't force a single word out of his mouth, no matter how hard he tried.

Kapil sat beside them, looking equally helpless as Renuka. He whispered fearfully to Renuka, "The medicine shop refused to give these pills with an outdated prescription. They need a new one."

Renuka stifled a sob and held Vihaan's hand. The burn inside Vihaan intensified as he looked at his parents now. The sight of them looking broken was the biggest punishment a son could get.

So, the three of them waited for Vihaan to get normal again. It took Vihaan almost three hours before he could move his body. Renuka's anxiety burst forth the moment she saw Vihaan stir, "How are you feeling?"

Vihaan stared at his parents for a moment and then broke down. "I don't want to live anymore."

Renuka threw her arms around Vihaan. "Don't say that! Never say that again."

Kapil put his hand on Vihaan's shoulder. His voice was determined when he spoke, "You want Tisha, right? Fine, I'll talk to her."

Vihaan could only stare at his father helplessly, tears spilling out of his eyes. A faint hope, the last straw kept Vihaan hanging by the thread.

The very next day Kapil set out for Mumbai to meet Tisha, while Ashwin and Renuka took Vihaan to a psychiatrist. The doctor didn't give a good prognosis. He was worried about Vihaan's state, so he advised Vihaan to take the pills in a higher dose whenever he felt too uncomfortable. Renuka and Ashwin didn't have words to console Vihaan. They only held each other tighter.

Vihaan came back home and got a call from his manager. He had skipped work without any notice right when he had been given so much responsibility. He had been dreading this call from the office, and he couldn't bring himself to receive it. The manager kept calling him all day, but he didn't respond. He couldn't even care about getting in trouble at work or even about getting fired. He stayed holed up in his room and Renuka kept him company all day, afraid of leaving him alone lest he had another panic attack with no one around to take care of him. And, she was right. The panic attacks kept coming that day, in differing intensities, for varying time periods, but each time it left Vihaan feeling weaker and more drained and more scared and more helpless than before.

Kapil returned home the next day with grave news. Tisha had refused to take Vihaan back into her life. She had said clearly that she couldn't fight with her father anymore and she couldn't disrupt her sister's life. Kapil had offered to talk to her father again, but she had not agreed to that either. The last hope Vihaan had, left him. None of them said anything, just sat together, sharing their silences. Vihaan tried with all his might not to think about Tisha, but she didn't leave his thoughts for a single moment, each memory sending a dart of poison through his whole being.

The next day, Kapil got a call from Vihaan's manager. Kapil explained the whole situation to the manager since

Vihaan was in no state to talk to anyone. Moreover, Vihaan knew fully well that his mental condition wouldn't be seen as conducive at the professional front, and this was distressing him even more, so Kapil didn't let Vihaan to go through these discussions in his fragile state. Kapil handled all the official negotiations on behalf of Vihaan. Vihaan's manager assured Kapil that Vihaan's condition would be considered. Within a week, things were settled at his office and he was given leave without pay for four months, and he was given permission to join the Hyderabad office whenever he wanted to start working again. This arrangement was completely out of the norm for an IT company, but Vihaan's colleagues were kind enough to stand with him in his hour of need.

As Vihaan stayed at home with his family, fighting with his regular panic attacks, life started losing all its colors. He had sketched out his life with Tisha to the minutest detail, and now nothing made any sense without her. Everything reminded him of her. His insides ached with every breath he took. The happiest memories of his London days came back to haunt him now. One minute he would tell himself that Tisha must be missing him, and then the next moment the reality would flood in, increasing the ache, the helplessness, the state of disbelief. Sometimes, the pain would become so severe that he would overdose on his medicines. His dosage of Clonazepam moved up from 0.5 mg to 5 mg. But slowly the medicines didn't seem to help his panic attacks even if he took 10 mg of Clonazepam.

Whenever Vihaan was alone, on sleepless nights or just at any time of the day, in the middle of any and every activity, he was filled with unbearable rage, at himself, at Tisha, at the society. He had seen in Rehan's case how Tisha could be whimsical and how unreasonable her father was, and yet he had jumped into the fray without thinking of the consequences. He was realizing only now how blinded he had been by his feelings for Tisha. Tisha had cheated on Rehan, and he should have known that of course, she could betray him too in some way. He didn't know who had more to be blamed for, Tisha, her father, or himself. But one moment, he would be blaming Tisha and the very next moment, he would be aching to see her again, to be with her again. He would find himself thinking of the most improbable ways of getting back with Tisha. He would keep imagining scenarios where he would be with her again. He kept wondering if Tisha was happy with the new guy in her life. Even though Tisha had moved on, but he couldn't entertain the thought of another relationship. The place he had given to Tisha, he could not bear to give that place to someone else. He would cry for hours. His parents would sometimes catch him in the act and try to calm him, but he kept begging them to let him cry. He saw the helplessness on his parents' faces when he broke down like that, and it made everything much much worse. He would stay in bed all day, not getting up even to eat.

On the loneliest of nights, he found himself writing poems again.

कुछ वादे किये थे हमने,
जो भुलाना चाहता हूँ,
तेरे साथ बिताये थे जो पल,
वो अब मिटाना चाहता हूँ,
इस महफ़िल में इसलिए आया मैं,
क्योंकि आज,
आज तुझे कुछ बताना चाहता हूँ।
जिस मोड़ पे तू छोड़ कर गई,

जिन वादों को तू तोड़ के गई,
क्या तुझे ज़रा सा भी इल्म है इसका?
कि हमारे रिश्ते को कैसे तू तोड़ कर गई।

Let me tell you

मेरी जात को तूने
मेरा गुनाह बना दिया,
जो मेरे हाथ में था ही नहीं,
उसी को वजह बना दिया।
बार–बार मिन्नतें कीं,
कोई और वजह बता दे,
जात कौन देखता है अब,
तू ये मुझे बता दे।
कुछ ऐसी वजह देती,
जिसपे मैं कुछ कर पाता,
मेरी कमी होती जो कोई
तो शायद उसे मैं सुधार पाता।
ऐसा नहीं था कि मुझे पता नहीं था,
समाज के दस्तूर से वाकिफ तो मैं भी था
और इसलिए हमने लड़ने की ठानी थी,
पर आधे रास्ते में छोड़कर जाना,
ये तो तेरी मनमानी थी।

Tisha was a part of him, a part that had come to define him, and with every passing day, he realized with even more certainty that Tisha would never really leave his heart. As this realization started becoming stronger, he became even more desperate to get rid of her memories. He gathered the courage and collected all the gifts Tisha had given him and went to Mumbai to leave them with the security guard at Tisha's apartment. After that, he felt lighter in a way he couldn't explain, though the peaceful feeling didn't last for too long before the anxieties creeped back in. He didn't stay in Mumbai even for one day, dreading the memories that lay hidden in every nook and corner of his life in Mumbai.

But even then, nothing helped. Tisha's memories were not tied to the materialistic life. They were inside him, a part of him, and it felt like getting rid of those memories would be like getting rid of himself. He understood and knew everything that his friends and family tried to tell him, but there was nothing Vihaan could do to ease his situation.

Every day some new symptoms would develop in his body, leaving him more panicked than before. He consulted some other doctors, but everyone said the same thing. Vihaan had to learn to control himself, and he had no idea how to do that. He saw his family members try their best to keep him company and cheer him up, and he pretended to go along with them just to keep them happy, but everyone knew that nothing was working. He was fighting two battles at once–the one inside him where he was trying not to succumb to his agony and the one outside where he had to act normal for his family. There would be nights when Vihaan would be dying of thirst but he couldn't move because of his panic attack. His parents slept beside him now, but slowly he stopped waking them up in the middle of the night, learning to hide his condition. Slowly he was starting to lose weight drastically and he became paler than usual. He developed a gaunt look in his eyes that made it impossible for him to even look at himself in the mirror.

His friends called him sometimes, but most often he ignored their calls and isolated himself from the world. One day his brother-in-law came to visit him. He said that whatever had happened to him was normal; that was how the society worked. So, he advised him to forget everything and get back to regular life. Vihaan kept quiet and listened to him, realizing how far he had been pushed from his acquaintances. Everyone saw his condition, but no one related to him anymore, nor did he feel any connection to anyone anymore. The feeling of loneliness kept stifling him more severely than he could ever explain. Everybody kept asking him what he wanted to do next, and he had only one answer to every question, "I don't know." Everyone said he would get better, that things would improve with time, but it just made him scoff to himself. The once bright and resourceful Vihaan was now aimless and lost. He could see this thought on every face around him and he agreed with them silently.

It was on the eve of his birthday in January when he kept wondering if Tisha would wish him. He kept waiting for her call, but it didn't come. His thoughts took him back to his last two birthdays, and the happy memories were excruciating now. That night as he was lost in his old memories, he had the idea of writing everything in a book. He sat with his laptop in the middle of the night, typing. But by the time he had reached two thousand words, he was feeling drained. He couldn't make himself relive all those romantic moments; he couldn't take himself back to the beginning. He sat blankly in front of his laptop and then gave up. He switched off his laptop and went to sleep.

When he woke up in the afternoon and went out of his room, he found his brother setting out to get a cake for his mother's birthday which was just one day after his birthday. Vihaan was surprised. "Why are you getting mom's cake one day early?"

Ashwin looked at him dubiously. "Today is mom's birthday."

Vihaan could only stare in shock. He checked his phone, and it was indeed his mother's birthday. He had missed a whole day in between and he couldn't understand what had happened. After his mother had cut her cake and Vihaan was alone with his father, he plucked up the courage to ask Kapil what had happened the previous day.

Kapil said, staring anxiously at Vihaan, "You slept all day."

"Oh!" Vihaan was taken aback. "You didn't wake me up?"

"We did," Kapil said, getting more worried now. "We had to splash water on your face to wake you up. Then your mother fed you and your brother brought your cake. You cut the cake. And, then you went to bed again."

Vihaan sat gaping at his father.

"You don't remember anything?" Kapil asked, horrified.

Vihaan shook his head. Kapil took him to the doctor that very evening. The doctor confirmed that Vihaan's state was deteriorating. And, from that day, apart from all the earlier symptoms, Vihaan started having short-term memory loss quite often. Sometimes, he would find cigarette burns on his hands and he wouldn't know how that had happened. Slowly, he started realizing that he was burning himself without being aware of his actions. He could see how stressed his parents were and he hid all this from his family. He didn't want to increase the burden on them. It was his age to look after his parents. And instead, he had stopped earning and had become completely dependent on his parents. The guilt, the shame started eating him up with passing time.

It was in the middle of February when he found out on social media that Bali was engaged to Kshitij. Something snapped inside him. Without thinking of anything he pinged Kshitij on his social media account and told him that he had been responsible for his break up with Tisha. He warned Kshitij that the Shuklas were whimsical and unreliable. He wrote how what happened to him. He let out all his frustration and hurt in that one message.

Two days later, Kapil got a call directly from Tisha. She was angry because Vihaan's message had created an uproar. Bali's relationship with Kshitij had come on the line.

Kapil stormed into Vihaan's room and hollered at him, "What have you done?"

Vihaan was clueless for a moment.

Kapil showed him his phone. "Tisha has called. Why did you try to ruin her sister's life?"

A fire leapt inside him. Vihaan demanded, "Disconnect that call first. Then we can talk."

"Tisha wants to talk to you." Kapil gave the phone to Vihaan.

"Hello, Vihaan?" After all these days, Vihaan was hearing Tisha's voice again. She was simply angry. There was no other emotion in her voice. And, the hurt deepened within him. "What have you done?"

"I just told the truth," Vihaan said, his voice amazingly calm.

Tisha's rage was boiling over. "It wasn't your place to talk."

"No, it wasn't," Vihaan agreed. "But was I given a chance to talk when it was my life on the line? Nothing is fair in this world."

"None of it was my fault, and you can't punish my sister for it," Tisha berated him harshly.

"None of this was my fault either, and still I was punished so badly," Vihaan countered her.

Tisha was speechless for a moment.

"What is Kshitij saying?" Vihaan asked, trying to control his temper.

Tisha explained, "We didn't tell Kshitij that he is responsible for our break up. We just said that we did it mutually because of my father didn't approve our relationship."

"That's only half the truth, Tisha," Vihaan said mercilessly. "And, it's worse than a lie."

"I don't care, Vihaan," Tisha was equally adamant. "There was no other choice but to say this, otherwise Kshitij would have backed out of the relationship. We couldn't let that happen." Tisha was desperate.

"What do you want now?" Vihaan asked her.

"Apologise to Kshiitij," Tisha demanded.

"Fine," Vihaan acquiesced. "But stop calling my father. If you have any problem, call me. I'll deal with you. I never dragged your parents in my mess. You have no right to do that either," Vihaan made himself very clear. There was no hesitation in his voice as he spoke to Tisha, knowing deep down that this might probably be the last time he was ever talking to her.

Tisha promised never to disturb him again and disconnected the call. His friends also learned about this incident and they all started saying how disappointed they were in him; especially his friend Aanchal was very vocal about her disappointment. Vihaan wanted to ask only one question to all these people: they were sermonising when he had done something wrong, but where were they when something wrong was being done to him? No one had anything to say when he threw this question at them, and Vihaan only smirked to himself as they squirmed. There were a lot of realities about his friends, about the society that he was learning, and he absorbed it all in like indelible lessons. Soon, Vihaan apologized to Kshitij, but the latter didn't get back to him again. He never learned what happened to Bali's relationship after that, and he stopped caring.

But this incident made Vihaan even more restless. One night he got very drunk and he ended up calling Tisha. Tisha was displeased to get a call from him in the dead of night. "Why are you calling me like this?"

Vihaan slurred, "We used to talk all night before? Remember? What happened to us?"

Tisha's voice became rougher. "There is no point in discussing the past, Vihaan."

"You are talking as if none of this matters to you," Vihaan accused her.

Tisha was silent.

"You miss me, Tisha, don't you?" Vihaan said pleadingly, hopefully.

"Vihaan, please, don't do this," she was getting sterner.

"Couldn't we give it another try, Tisha? I can't live without you, Tisha. I can't," Vihaan said desperately.

Without a reply, Tisha disconnected the call. The next morning when Vihaan started coming back to his senses, a feeling of shame and guilt engulfed him.

But after this debacle, a tie got snapped in Vihaan, and it was snapped for good. It felt like he was emerging from deep water and that he could breathe deeply again. The texture of his thoughts started changing color. Earlier it was disbelief and hurt over a broken relationship. Something that was the ultimate truth to him had been turned into the biggest lie. And, he had been struggling to let that lie sink inside him. Now, what troubled him most was the insult. Tisha's father didn't think his family had the standard just because of their caste. All his life he had seen his parents and his siblings work hard and live a peaceful, respectable life. But suddenly none of that mattered. Every idea that had been inculcated in him about life and society was shattered now. And, he was struggling to come to terms with this ugly facet of the society where human beings were still judged on things like caste. The sting of injustice would sometimes become so strong inside him that it suffocated him.

Since Vihaan had stopped living an active life, so his family members tried to get him involved in some interesting activities, but he never agreed to get out of bed. The three lakh rupees he had saved to buy a diamond ring for Tisha were still lying in his bank account. He started spending that money on his family members.

He was drinking and smoking way more than he had ever done. Soon, he had blown up all his savings and he was penniless. But it didn't bother him any. He realized his behavior might make it seem like he was becoming a drunkard, but he didn't really care. The drinks took him into a haze where he stopped feeling anything for a little while, and he welcomed that blissful oblivion more than anything.

One night he came home heavily drunk and he wanted to have a good sleep, so he ended up swallowing the pills that were meant to last for a week. Then he fell on his bed and was lost to the world immediately. But around 3 a.m. he woke up, feeling very uncomfortable and soon he started vomiting. After that he couldn't fall asleep at all and stayed up all night, thinking about all the horrible things he had been doing to himself, feeling worse than ever, and that is when he resolved to try harder and be saner from then on.

What now made him feel peaceful was staying at home and talking to his family and helping them in whatever little ways he could. His family kept suggesting different ideas because they felt if he focused on something productive, it would help him. They said he should get a new job or get a PR for Australia or Canada and shift there. All these ideas were great, but all of these would lead Vihaan back to IT, and he felt like that part of his life was over. He didn't feel there was anything more than he wanted to achieve. It had been almost four months since he had been sitting at home, and he had no idea what he was seeking. But one thing he knew for sure, whatever it was that he needed, he wasn't going to find it in IT.

Vihaan kept all his thoughts to himself because he knew no one would understand what he was talking about. They would all think Vihaan had gone mad. No one said it directly, but Vihaan understood nonetheless. His symptoms and his behavior seemed odd to everyone, and no one related to him, and all of it made him feel more and more isolated. Over the course of his illness, there were moments when Vihaan wanted to share his thoughts and his agonies with someone, but he knew everyone was busy in their lives and he didn't want to bother anyone with his problems.

His health wasn't improving drastically, but he was learning something new and something invaluable every single day as he struggled on with himself.

The thought of joining the office at Hyderabad started crossing his mind again. But he didn't feel strong enough yet. His family members didn't ever make him feel uncomfortable about the fact that he was not earning, but he started thinking about it more and more. He started realizing that the needs inside him had changed. Even a year back he was just a young man who wanted to make a nice and comfortable life for himself and his family. But he had been stripped of his self-worth, his sense of identity, and now he needed to prove his worth to himself. He hadn't been considered worthy just because of his lower caste. Now he wanted to show himself what he could achieve if he set his heart to it. And along with that, he wanted to bring a shift in the unjust beliefs that had ruined his life. He wanted to show people how wrong these orthodox ideas were and he wanted to try and make a better society where such evil beliefs wouldn't ruin someone else's life. He wanted to stand in front of the whole world and scream out to them: Judge a man by his character, not his caste. He wanted to raise his voice against the injustice that had been meted out to him. But it was getting the right platform that was going to be the challenge. He knew what he wanted was a distant goal, a need to which he knew no path, a need he couldn't even visualize clearly, and yet this need started building and growing inside him, just the way love for Tisha had grown inside of him one day. The UPSC examinations started feeling like the ultimate aim in his life because if he could become an IAS officer it would give him an identity of his own, it would make people listen to him; he would be taken seriously. It would give him credibility, it could bring in the platform that he needed to highlight issues of such orthodox mentality.

But he knew this was going to be no mean feat since this was the most difficult examination in the country, and due to the age limits, he could just give this his two tries. It was a long shot, but this idea seemed to get a hold over him. He mulled over this idea for a few days and found himself browsing online to learn more about these examinations, the syllabus, the books, the older question papers, the mock tests. The more he researched the more he felt a belief within him. There was some inexplicable intuition working in his heart that told him he could do it. He knew if he could achieve this, then this could show Tisha's father that caste doesn't define or limit anyone's abilities and standard. By then, of course, Tisha would be married to someone else, but he still wanted to show the people who had judged him and discarded him so unfairly that the wheel of fortune rotated, and nothing in life was fixed. He had had enough of playing the blame game with God. He wanted to get justice, and he felt a new determination to get it in his own way. The way he had fought for his love, he was going to fight for himself now, he promised himself.

One day he told his family members about his decision. They were elated when they heard that Vihaan was thinking about his life again. Everyone encouraged him to go ahead, though they also pointed out the pitfalls. But Vihaan had already considered everything, and he reassured them that this was something he really wanted to do.

But even with his heart set on this, there was something amiss in his heart, something that was making him restless. His love couldn't become the reality, but he didn't want it to fail either. He knew his love was true and he didn't want it to get lost in the realm of forgotten darkness. The idea that had been niggling within him for some time now had to be explored before he could focus on other things. So, he took his laptop to his room, and opened up a Word file to type the title page of his book:

My Only Sin Is My Caste

A message for society:

प्यार–प्यार है उसे प्यार ही रहने दो,
अपने सोच के दायरे से मत बाँधो इसे,
ये आज़ाद है इसे आज़ाद ही रहने दो।